Red R

th

Witch's Thread

VICTORIA WILLIAMSON

Silver Thistle Press

This edition published by Silver Thistle Press Ltd in 2024

Silver Thistle Press Ltd
272 Bath Street,
Glasgow
G2 4JR

For all enquiries, please email: enquiries@silverthistlepress.com
www.silverthistlepress.com

978-1-7384364-2-2

Printed in Great Britain

This book is dedicated with thanks to the staff and volunteers of the Paisley Book Festival whose hard work and enthusiasm helped launch it.

Broken Threads:

Friday 1st June 1722 - Morning

The skein of thread that lay in the merchant's beefy hand was white against his mottled flesh, the twisted fibres spun fine as silk and bleached over many months. As she watched the linen dealer hold the strands up to the light, testing their strength by pulling them between his stubby fingers, Christian felt suddenly queasy. It wasn't the contrast between the loving care she'd poured into her work and the rough treatment her sample was receiving, or even the sight of the merchant's blackened nails picking at her fine spinning that turned her stomach. In the bright morning sunshine streaming through the office windows, Christian could see the full effect of her laborious bleaching process on the skein of thread. It was her best effort yet, almost rivalling the finest linen she'd seen in Holland during her trip last autumn.

Almost...

She wanted her thread white as the first snows of winter, but this fresh batch had the pale cast of curdled milk – white, yes, but not white enough.

"I've seen better." The merchant's beady eyes narrowed, hiding his admiration for her work behind a mask of indifference. "And I've seen whiter. This is the best I can offer." He threw the skein down on the dusty counter and scribbled a figure on a scrap of paper. Christian glanced at it, and felt the bile rise in her throat again. She'd getter a better price selling piecemeal to the wives of the tenant farmers on her family's estate.

Beside her, Christian could feel her maid's body stiffen in indignation. Meg knew better than to speak her mind in front of her betters, but it was taking every ounce of her self-control not to stand up for the mistress she'd served for so long.

"Thank you, Master Ferguson, but I know the worth of my labour better than you do, it seems, and I'll take it where it's better appreciated."

Christian saw a flicker of hesitation in the merchant's eyes as she picked up her fine skein and placed it in her bag, and for a moment she hoped he'd reconsider. But then he simply shrugged and said, "You'll not get a better price in all of Paisley for a woman's work. Good day to you, Widow Millar."

As he turned away to sort his pile of ledgers, she heard it. The word that had haunted her since her childhood, the stain that no amount of washing and

and bleaching could ever cleanse. “We want none of your witch’s thread here, anyway,” was what she was sure the merchant muttered under his breath. The sour taste in Christian’s mouth made her gag, and she clutched Meg’s wrist, hurrying her out of the office before the maid could speak her mind.

As soon as they were out on the street once more, Meg gave full rein to her resentment. “Well!” she snorted. “Did you ever hear the like? ‘Woman's work’ he called it, as if your clever hands don’t spin the finest thread in the whole of Scotland! Taking liberties, he is. He wouldn’t have dared to talk to you like that if your poor brothers were still living, God rest their souls.”

Christian let her maid prattle on, heedless of Meg’s angry rant. The blood was pounding in her ears, drumming out a single dreadful word that thundered up from the depths of her memory and drowned out every other sound.

Witch.

Witch.

WITCH!

An ale merchant’s wagon passed by in a blur, the horse’s hooves echoing the reproach as they beat out a damning tattoo on the cobblestones.

Witch, witch, witch, witch, witch....

“Did you hear what he muttered under his breath?” Meg’s voice finally grew shrill enough to cut through the noise in Christian's head. "A pox on him for his vicious tongue. After everything you suffered through to bring the wicked of this world to justice,and you a minister's widow too. What sinful slander! I've not met a more God-fearing soul as you in all my forty-four years, Mistress Shaw."

Mistress Shaw. Even now, Meg still called her by the name she'd had all those years ago, during the time of the trials. The name that had become infamous: Christian Shaw, the child who'd been bewitched.

"And as for that fat old swindler saying your thread wasn't white enough for the likes of him!" Meg scoffed. "Why, even that fancy linen we saw in Amsterdam wasn't as fine as yours, Mistress Shaw."

"He's right," Christian said sharply, pulling herself together by sheer force of will and closing her mind to the sound of distant drumming. "It's not white enough. I haven't perfected the bleaching process yet. Come, Meg, we have work to do."

Seeing the determination etched into the face of her mistress, Meg bit her tongue and followed Christian obediently, contenting herself with throwing contemptuous scowls back at the office building as they hurried away.

The west end of Paisley was humming with activity, the road full of traders' wagons and townsfolk jostling for space as the snorting horses jogged past. Hawkers' cries echoed through the streets, competing with the clang of blacksmiths' hammers and the rumble of cartwheels. Maids carrying baskets of fresh laundry gathered by the courtyards' back entrances to gossip in the morning sunshine. Young boys whistled their way through the throng, their arms laden with meat, eggs, and sacks of oatmeal they'd fetched from market.

Christian saw and heard none of the life of the town. Her mind was fixed on one task only: return home to Bargarran House and find a way to make her thread even whiter. With her head full of bleaching methods, she barely noticed that her feet were carrying her up High Street towards the Gallow Green. It wasn't until Meg grasped the end of her blue plaid, urging her to choose a different path, that she realised where she was going.

"Not that way, mistress." Meg shook her head. "Thomas is waiting for us down at the fish market with the horse and cart. "It'll be quicker if we go the other way round the Tollbooth."

Christian knew she was right, but somehow she couldn't make her feet change course. It was as though an unseen force was pulling her towards the spot she'd last visited nearly twenty-five years before, and she was powerless to resist. Each unwilling step brought her closer to the barren waste ground where convicts were hanged before a throng of baying spectators. In her dreams she still heard the shouts of 'Witch! Witch!' as a row of victims was strangled one by one.

The taunts hadn't been thrown at her that day, but at those she'd accused, those she'd condemned. And ever since, the word had haunted her every waking moment, whispered in the street, muttered behind hands, and carried on the wind on dark winter nights.

Despite the warmth of the sun, Christian shuddered as she gazed at the patches of scorched earth where the grass had never grown back, even after all this time. Cursed, the townfolk said. There had been no witch burnings since that terrible day, but the ground remembered, the weeds shrivelled to blanched yellow stalks to mark the site where the pyres had once blazed.

The flames were red, Christian thought, the memory burned into her brain. And the bodies were blackened like charred oatbread by the time it was over. Such a terrible smell...

"Come away, mistress, we shouldn't linger here," Meg fretted, plucking at Christian's plaid again. The long length of cloth draped over her shoulder and across her arm was too heavy for such a bright day, but Christian felt her skin turn cold as ice under the thick blue tartan. She clutched at the heavy silver crucifix hanging from her neck as images flashed through her head, seared into her mind like jagged scars of lightning.

An old woman's eyes fixed on hers, pleading for mercy, then turning dark with fear and rage as the executioner's rope tightened around her throat.

A wild shriek silencing the crowd for a long moment before the rope was pulled taut.

'May you never know peace until the day you die!'

And the strange sight of a huge black raven fluttering down to perch on the stake the woman was chained to, its head cocked to one side as it watched the body below twitch and gasp its last.

"Mistress, please?" Meg was close to begging, more frightened now by Christian's pale face than by the legends of this place of the damned. "People are staring at us."

Roused in an instant, Christian glanced round. An old man in a labourer's smock muttered a prayer as he passed by. A young woman in a silk dress crossed the street to avoid the spot by the gallows where Christian stood. A group of servants whispered behind their hands, their eyes darting to the ground when Christian met their gaze. She knew their stories weren't just of the Bargarran witches. The stories were about her.

"Yes, let's go," Christian said, sickened by the stares as much as by the memories. "Let's go home."

She let Meg take her arm as they left the site of suffering, walking now with purposeful steps back to the cart and their transport home. But Christian couldn't help glancing back as they passed Maxwellton Cross. Her eyes were drawn against her will to the spot where the witches were buried. Their unmarked grave was topped by a single horseshoe, the witch-warding standing as a silent testament to their sins in the eyes of God. It was where the ashes of all seven she'd condemned were laid to rest, strangled by the executioner's noose before being burned at the stake. The eighth had escaped his terrible fate by strangling himself in his cell, but his death weighed no less heavily on her conscience.

They were guilty! Christian told herself, forcing herself to stand firm against the tide of memories that threatened to drown her. *They all deserved their fate.*

Hadn't they..?

Christian gasped. On the mound of scrubby grass lay a snow-white dove, its breast laid open, blood staining its feathers. A monstrous raven loomed over its kill, its beak stained red. Tilting its head, it looked straight at Christian.

From where she stood, the raven appeared to be smiling.

Weft:

Monday 4th June 1722

The workroom was almost silent. The two servant girls Christian had trained to slackly twist the flax threads before their first bleaching were bent over their wheels, deep in concentration. Their feet and hands moved in steady motion as they pumped the treadles and teased the yellow fibres out into long strings that wrapped around the whirling spindles. They were good workers, and they were obedient. If there had been one lasting outcome of the witch trials, it was that Christian never had any problems with servants challenging her authority.

No one dared.

Still, she wouldn't trust the delicate work of spinning the partly-bleached string into fine thread to anyone except herself and her sisters, and even then, she had to keep a close eye on them to ensure their work was up to her exacting standards.

"Elizabeth!" she called sharply, seeing her sister wet her fingers in her mouth instead of the small bowl of water at her elbow. "How many times do I have to tell you not to spit on the thread? It's disgusting!"

Elizabeth threw her a sour look. At thirty-two she was five years younger than Christian, but her pinched face and grey eyes that were clouded with resentment made her seem the elder of the two. It wasn't just Christian whose name had been whispered through town since her childhood. The whole Shaw family had been tainted, and Elizabeth wore the bitterness that came with being passed over for marriage by all the eligible bachelors of their acquaintance on her face like battle wounds. Christian's brief marriage to Reverend Millar had sent her younger sister into paroxysms of jealousy, and since his death last year and her return to the family home, Christian had barely had a single civil word out of her. But Elizabeth was a skilled spinner, and for the sake of the family business she hoped to one day build, Christian made an effort to keep the peace.

Except, of course, when Elizabeth was breaking her strict rules on cleanliness.

"Use the water bowl to wet the thread," Christian insisted. "We'll never get it white enough if you keep fouling it."

"What difference does it make?" Elizabeth shot back. "This is the way I've always done it, and it'll go through another bleaching afterwards anyway. We all know well enough it's not the whiteness of the thread that's making it hard to sell in town."

Christian felt the muscles in her jaw clench. It was a direct challenge, and Elizabeth should know better than to talk to her like that in front of the servants. Before she could think of a suitable rebuke, the door flew open and their youngest sister, Jean, came running in.

"You'll never guess what!" she cried, giddy with excitement and heedless of the quiet of the workroom. At twenty-six, she was past her first bloom of youth, but she'd grown into the long limbs and wild hair that had given her the look of a startled colt when she was eighteen. Now, with her plump cheeks and her chestnut hair tamed into smooth braids, she was all the prettier for the extra years. Elizabeth's scowl deepened as she looked up at her beaming sister. Jean clearly had good news, and that meant a fresh reason for envy was about to be announced.

"You remember Alexander Murray, who inherited the family estate in Kilbarchan last year?" she asked breathlessly. Christian nodded, her hands folded serenely in her lap as she waited for the rest of the news. Elizabeth's only reply was a long snort of feigned contempt.

"Well, he—"

"The most wonderful news!" their mother interrupted,

shuffling in a good twenty paces behind Jean. It wasn't her three score years and more that was making the climb up the stairs difficult these days, but her fondness for plum puddings and sweet wine. "Alexander Murray is coming to visit!" she panted, stealing her daughter's thunder. "He's returned from his Grand Tour of Europe, and will be coming to call on us the day after next."

"And why," Elizabeth said through gritted teeth, "is that good news for us? We've little enough beef as it is, without having to feed unwanted guests."

The Bargarran estate had once been rich, but their father was long dead, and without the ninth Laird's strong hand on the family purse strings, the ensuing debts and financial entanglements had taken years to unravel. After the early demise of his sons, the farm had suffered from neglect, and the daughters had to turn to their own clever hands to make up the shortfall.

"Hush, Lizzie!" their mother chided. "For a man such as Alexander Murray we'll find collops and roast hens enough to feed a king's army, isn't that right, Christian?" Their mother looked to her eldest daughter hopefully.

"He can come, can't he, Chrissy?" Jean urged.

"You know we don't have enough in the larder for a dinner on that scale, don't you, Christian?" Elizabeth made sure to add her opinion.

Christian stared back at the eyes that were all turned to her expectantly. *Why is it always up to me?* she wondered. Everyone was always waiting for her to make a decision. Waiting for her to give her opinion before agreeing. Waiting to make sure it was *safe* to speak.

"We're not in such straits that we can't give a returning neighbour the welcome back home he deserves," she said, earning the relieved sigh of her mother and a smile of eternal gratitude from her youngest sister. "And if we are," she added with emphasis for Elizabeth's sake, "then we'd best not show it."

"I'll go down and pick out the fattest hens right now!" Jean called over her shoulder as she rushed out, her feet pattering down the stairs at top speed.

Her delight was almost more than Elizabeth could bear. "Why must we entertain that empty-headed fop when our meat is in such short supply?" she grumbled. "He has near half the cows and hens in Scotland on his own estate – let him dine at home and be done with it."

"My dear," their mother sighed, "it's precisely *because* our meat is in short supply, and he has an estate stuffed full of cows and hens, that we must entertain him."

"Janet, Bess – take the spindles down to the bleaching green," Christian said quickly. "I want the next batch ready for spinning as soon as possible." She waited until the servant girls had left the room before showing her displeasure. "Mother, why must you always be so indiscreet in front of the servants?"

"Who's indiscreet?" their mother blustered. "I'm not saying anything about the state of our finances that every tenant family in Bargarran doesn't already know. And as for Alexander Murray, well! All of Paisley knows he's fond of our Jeanie. He would have proposed you know, before he left for his Grand Tour, if you hadn't been so disapproving."

"Me?" Christian was genuinely surprised. "I barely exchanged ten words with him before we left for Holland. I said nothing to him that might be considered a discouragement."

"Not to *him*, no, but you know how much Jeanie values your opinion. She wouldn't have been so lukewarm to him if you'd even hinted you thought him a worthy young man."

"Mother, I know well enough what a marriage to a man of such means is worth to our whole family, regardless of what I think of him personally. If they both like each other, then there's nothing I can do to put either of them off the idea, is there?"

"No, of course not," Elizabeth interrupted, her lip twisted in disgust. "You've never done anything that would put suitors off courting your sisters, have you?"

"Lizzie, dear," their mother said wearily, "it's that curdled look your face insists on wearing that puts suitors off, not anything that might have happened many years in the distant past."

There was silence for a long moment, the unpleasant period of family history that was never spoken of aloud hanging heavy in the air between them. It was shattered by Elizabeth pushing her stool back petulantly, its wooden legs screeching across the floorboards. "Well, if Jean thinks she's got your permission to feed our whole henhouse to that prancing fool, she'll have most of their necks wrung already. I'd best go and rein her in before she butchers the lot."

Her silk gown rustled as she swept out of the workroom, leaving the faint impression behind that a storm had passed overhead without breaking. An awkward silence ensued when Lady Shaw realised she'd been left quite alone with her eldest daughter. Christian could almost feel her mother shrinking from her, as though finding herself face to face with a snake she suspected might well be poisonous.

"Well then, I'll let you get back to your work," Lady Shaw said hurriedly, heading for the door. Christian was just about to return to her spinning, when her mother suddenly turned back again. "I nearly forgot! I've been building a trousseau for Jean – just some little things to add to the chest. I've been saving the best linen for years."

Christian didn't question why her mother hadn't given her the finest family linen on her marriage to Reverend Millar. She'd know since she was a child that she was her mother's least favourite, and even Elizabeth in the throes of her worst tantrums seemed preferable to Lady Shaw than Christian's company.

"Perhaps you could finish this for me?" Lady Shaw held up a delicate linen cap with a frilled front. "Your needlework is much finer than mine, and I do so want it to be perfect."

"Mother, that's a baby's cap," Christian protested when she saw how small it was.

"And what if it is?" her mother said a little defensively. "There's nothing wrong with hoping for grandchildren, is there? A baby would breathe fresh life into this old house. We've not heard the cries of a babe under this room since our Jeanie herself was born."

Christian felt a strange reluctance to take the small piece of linen, but her mother was insistent. She felt something sharp cut her palm as Lady Shaw pressed it into her hand, but her mother was in too much of a hurry to escape her eldest daughter's oppressive presence to notice. As the door shut with a thump, Christian dropped the white christening cap into her lap and pulled at the sewing needle that had been accidentally thrust into her hand.

At the sight of the small drops of blood welling in her palm and dripping onto the pure white linen of the cap, Christian felt suddenly dizzy. Her vision blurred, and she heaved herself to her feet, staggering to the window.

I just need air! she told herself, fumbling with the window sash. Her hands were sweating, and the small smear of red in her palm seemed to blossom until it filled her whole vision. Unable to open the window, she pressed her forehead against the cool glass instead, trying to catch her breath. The red haze swirled to the edges of her vision, and through the narrow tunnel in its centre, she saw a terrible sight. On the sill outside, a raven was watching her, its eyes glistening like black mirrors. Opening its beak, it let loose one terrible caw that sounded like the wail of an infant.

Somewhere, somewhen in the distant past, someone was crying.

Christian sank to the floor, her whole body shaking as she remembered.

Warp:

Wednesday 10th June 1697

I'm standing in the hall where I shouldn't be, where I've been told *not to be*, but no one has noticed because they're all in there with Mama, too busy trying to keep her from dying.

She screams again and the sound goes right through me.

I cling to the door, peering into the bedroom where the women are working. Meg is pouring fresh well water into a bowl, and Kitty's pressing a damp cloth to Mama's head. Mama is sitting up in bed, her shoulders pulled tight with pain like she's being squeezed from the inside out. There's another figure bending down, lost for a moment in the shadows. The candlelight flickers again, and a huge shadow is cast on the wall as the figure straightens up. I can see a pointed beak like a raven, and long twitching feathers that look like knives.

There's a rag tied to the end of the bed, and it's red, red, red like the blood on the figure's hands as they go plunging beneath my mother's nightdress. Her cries are coming louder and faster now, and I can feel each shriek cutting a fresh slice off my skin, leaving me so raw and exposed that each breath of air I gasp out feels like fire on my face.

The raven shadow isn't a bird, but an old woman with a pointed nose and busy hands, but the candles are flickering and Mama is screaming and I'm so frightened I can't see straight.

There's a final scream so loud I'm sure Mama is dead and gone to hell, as no one flying to heaven would make a sound so terrible. The shadows on the wall twist, and a bloody bundle is held up to the light – a pile of meaty limbs like the butcher's castoffs when he's done his work in the cowshed. But this raw meat is squirming like it's alive, and Mama is whimpering like she's not dead, and the blood is blossoming on the bed sheets and everything in the world is white linen stained with red under cover of darkness.

The feather fingers flap and slap and the monstrous bundle lets loose a wail that sounds like the cry of a bird, and I know I'm going to pass out as I haven't taken a breath in almost forever. I must have made a sound, though, as the pointed beak nose turns my way as though it can smell my fear. Meg and Kitty have taken the bundle of meat and are washing it in the bowl like it's a chicken plucked for the roast, and I can't see Mama as she's lying back on the bed where the shadows are deepest. I can hear her sobbing as the raven woman with blood on her hands wipes them on the red, red rag, and I don't know if Mama's crying because she's dying for real this time or she's afraid the old woman will hurt me the way she must have hurt her.

A face looms in the doorway, all wrinkled and lined like a gnarled tree trunk, and the raven woman with blood on her hands speaks. She says, "Don't worry, pet. I've tied a red rag to the bed for luck, and it'll work its charm to stop the bleeding."

But the blood smeared on the rag is pounding in my head now, and I'm running, running, running to the beat of its drum. Running away from the red-white linen and the black shadows and the raven woman with the feather fingers that have cut my world into little pieces. As I run through the dark to my room I can hear a bird crying, or maybe it's the bundle of squirming meat, as the sound is too shrill to be Mama.

I throw myself down by my bed and I clasp my hands to pray, pray, pray until my throat is raw with whispering and the words feel heavy on my tongue. I don't hear the servant come in until she's standing right next to me, her candle making firelight dance on the floorboards. I look up and hope it's Meg come to hold me and comfort me and put me to bed with kisses, but it's not, it's Katherine Campbell with the curly hair that's red, red, red as bundles and rags. Katherine is sharp and spiky and tells me to stop snivelling and be grateful that my mother has lived and I've got a new baby sister just come into this world.

I'm confused and muddled now, as I thought babies were gifts from God that were carried down from heaven on the wings of angels, and I don't know what the raven woman and the squirming meat in the dark have to do with my new sister.

Katherine laughs her nasty laugh deep in her throat like the caw of a bird and tells me I need to grow up as I'm eleven now and need to know about the facts of life. I know my Catechism and my ABCs and I'm starting to learn how to spin flax into thread, but I don't know how deep the well of evil runs in this world, or that Katherine wants to plunge me down into its murky depths.

Sitting on my bed and clutching my wrist so I can't run and hide from the truths that drip from her tongue like poison, she tells me things. Terrible things of what men and women do in the dark, and of the well of evil that's really a tunnel of sin down which the squirming meaty bundles are squeezed in the night with wailing cries. And then she tells me something more awful than anything I could ever imagine in my worst nightmares. She tells me that one day soon I'll be a woman too and I'll know for sure because there will be blood on my linen that's red, red, red and then I'll be

ready for the terrible things in the dark and the scarlet
rag on the bed when the raven woman comes calling.

Weft:

Monday 4th June 1722

It had been an effort to pick herself up off the floor after such a disturbing vision, but Christian was strong, and she wasn't about to let buried memories claw their way out of the innermost parts of her mind after all this time. With her family in such a precarious financial position, there was too much at stake, too much to lose, for her to give in to such unforgivable weakness.

Not now! Christian shouted to her subconscious, shutting the lid tight on the Pandora's box that had suddenly flown open. *Not when I'm so close to perfecting the bleaching process.*

She took a long, steadying breath, then marched down to the library to check on the progress of her latest batch of thread. It was called a 'library' more out of custom than actual function. There had never been many books on the shelves even in her father's time, and the ninth Laird of Bargarran had used it as an office during the day and a place of retreat in the evenings when he wanted to be alone with his thoughts by the fire.

Now Christian used it as an extension of her workroom, her ever-expanding industry evidenced by the skeins of thread lining the former bookshelves, labelled samples of her various experiments arranged like medical curiosities on an apothecary's shelf. As part of her bleaching process, most of the windows were blocked by large slates held in place by pegs attached to the window frames, throwing the library half into shadow. Christian passed along the rows of shelves, examining her specimens carefully in the dim light.

'November 2nd batch. First bleaching: 2 days steeped in vegetable lye, washed with soft white soap. Second bleaching: 2 days steeped in vegetable lye, washed with soft white soap, soaked in milk and water for 3 days.'

The sample attached to this label had a slight yellowish cast, the threads parting like the pages of an old book under Christian's touch. She threw the skein down in disgust and passed on along the rows of samples, pausing at one from a later date.

'January 5th batch. First bleaching: 3 days steeped

in vegetable lye, washed with soft white soap. Second bleaching: 3 days steeped in potash lye, washed with soft white soap, soaked in buttermilk for 3 days.'

This thread was whiter, taking on the hue of the buttermilk it had bathed in. Christian frowned. *Still not nearly pure enough.*

She stopped at a skein from her last batch, the one she'd tried to sell in Paisley the previous day.

'April 5th batch: First bleaching: 3 days steeped in potash lye, washed with soft white soap. Second bleaching: 3 days steeped in potash lye, washed with soft white soap, soaked in buttermilk for 4 days, exposed to sunlight for 6 weeks.'

This batch was the whitest yet, and the strong threads glowed in the sunbeam streaming through the exposed window above the desk. Yet to Christian's eyes it looked pale and sickly rather than clean, as though there were a disease at the very heart of her process.

Not pure enough yet for my machine, she sighed to herself, running her fingers over the components of metal and wood that lay in disassembled pieces on the shelves behind the great oak desk. Smuggling the machine parts out of Holland after her autumn fact-checking trip had been a real test of her courage, but somehow she'd managed it without being caught. Meg had taken a share of the contraband willingly enough at the request of her mistress, but her mother had to be bullied into carrying a piece of the machinery through the port, and her mother's maid had to be bribed before she would take the risk. It had been worth it, though.

Christian eyed the schematics laid on her father's desk – *her* desk – with satisfaction. The hand-powered twist mill that would allow a dozen spindles of her hand-spun linen to be twisted into strong thread all at once would revolutionise linen commerce in Scotland. It was no wonder the plans and machine parts were such a heavily guarded secret in Holland. But the secret was out, and if only Christian could get her thread white enough, then she'd be mistress of the fledgling industry just as it was ready to soar to great heights.

Christian Millar, thread manufacturer, she thought with a thrill of longing. It sounded so much better than 'Christian Shaw, the child who was bewitched.' She couldn't change her past, but this was her chance to change the way she'd be remembered by posterity.

She went to one of the windows and unclipped her small test slate to check the progress of her latest batch. The large slates required the help of several servants to manoeuvre, but she'd rigged up this small one to keep an eye on the final bleaching stage over the long weeks the sunlight needed to do its work. She tried not to check it every day – she tried *so* hard – but even her iron will was no match for the pull of the threads laid flat against the window pane.

She lifted the lengths of tightly twisted flax, holding them up to the light. They were whiter than the last batch, yes, but were they white *enough?*

"Christian?" Her mother's voice held the same note of trepidation that always irritated her whenever she heard it.

"I'm busy, mother. What is it now?"

Her mother made an elaborate show of tiptoeing into the room so as not to disturb the peace, a pantomime made more ridiculous by the thumping footsteps her portly frame couldn't help but make.

"We've been discussing Alexander Murray's visit," her mother said in a dramatic stage whisper, "and we thought that a dinner of roast hens might be a poor show for a man of such consequence. We were wondering, it perhaps a calf might be better..?"

It was phrased as a statement, but its tone, as always, implied a question.

"By 'we', I take it you mean yourself and Jean?" Christian said, even though she already knew the answer. Her mother rarely asked anything of Christian unless it was on behalf of her favourite daughter. In fact, her mother rarely spoke to her at all unless it was strictly necessary.

Their trip to Holland in the autumn had been a trial for them both, but as a widow still young enough to remarry, Christian had needed an older chaperone, and her mother was the only person she could browbeat into accompanying her. She had no friends, and no other relatives who wanted anything to do with her after the 'nasty business' of her childhood. She'd spent two months touring thread factories, linen production companies, bleaching fields and spinning workshops with Meg, leaving her mother to while away the long hours of her visits in nearby coffee houses with her own servant. Breakfast and suppers together had been a strain, but one Christian had been willing to endure to secure her precious machine parts and plans.

"Well, yes, myself and Jeanie," her mother laughed nervously, unsure if there was cause for rebuke in the admission. "But it needn't be a fine beast," she hurried on. "Thomas says the one that was lamed by the dog last month hasn't recovered, and if it's not going to grow healthily, then there's no harm in serving it up in a nice ragout, is there?"

"Mother, you are the Lady of this house. If you wish to slaughter a calf, then that's your decision to make, not mine."

"Yes, but all the same..." Her mother hesitated, twisting

her fingers together in that irritating way that reminded Christian of naughty children stumbling through their Catechism as they stood before a stern minister. Christian had always recited her Catechism and prayers flawlessly in her youth, earning her the praise of the local clergy and the admiration of her peers. She'd always been clever. She'd always been strong-willed and determined.

Except for that one time aged eleven, when her strength had failed her, and her mind had unravelled like threads flying off a broken spindle.

That was not my doing! she told herself, digging her fingers into her palm where the needle had pieced her skin, willing the memories to stay suppressed. *I was bewitched. I was under their spell, and I couldn't help myself. It was their own actions that damned them, not mine.*

Wasn't it..?

Maybe if her mother had been less timid and biddable, less prone to superstitious beliefs, she might have settled on a more rational explanation for her daughter's affliction. Maybe if her grandfather hadn't died in mysterious circumstances on a winter night in 1676, her own father might not have been so quick to transfer her case from doctors to the local clergy and seek a supernatural explanation. Maybe if Katherine Campbell had only reined in her loose tongue the night

Jean was born, none of the subsequent events would have unfolded with such tragic consequences.

So many poor decisions. So much suffering.

"Christian?" Her mother's apprehensive voice broke in on her thoughts. "Do you have a decision? About the calf?"

"Ask Thomas to slaughter it tomorrow. That will give Mary time to prepare the meat for Wednesday's dinner."

"Wonderful! I'll leave you to your work, then." Lady Shaw beamed, the relief evident in her face as she repeated her pantomime tiptoe in reverse order out of the door.

Christian sighed when the heavy footsteps faded down the hall. She found her mother's presence oppressive, yet she couldn't quite put her finger on why, even after all these years.

I must get back to work, she thought, promising herself to labour doubly hard at her spinning wheel to make up for her temporary weakness earlier. Crossing the long hallway to the stairs, she barely glanced at the deer heads and portraits hung on the walls high above her. Skinned animals made her shudder, and the faces of long-gone ancestors that glared down at her were worse. She'd had more than enough dreams of dead faces chained to stakes to last her a lifetime.

Lost in her thoughts, she nearly ran straight into a

young servant on the second floor who was just coming out of Jean's room carrying a large earthenware pot.

"Watch where you're going, you silly girl," Christian scolded. "How many times do you have to be told that the chamberpots are to be emptied first thing in the morning and late in the evening when the family are at supper? What if a visitor were to come upon you carrying one of those down the stairs?"

"Sorry, mistress," the girl said, her eyes fixed on the ground. She was far too timid to add that no one had visited Bargarran House for so long she might as well dance through the dining room with them in the middle of the day, but Christian knew that's what she was thinking.

"Well, hurry up, then. And don't let me catch you behind on your chores again," Christian said sternly. The girl nodded meekly and hurried away. Just as she reached the stairs, the cloth cover she'd laid across the chamber pot fell off, and she quickly caught it up again, throwing a nervous glance at Christian over her shoulder as she disappeared down the stairs. It took a moment for Christian to process what she'd seen, then the breath caught painfully in her throat.

The bowl had been filled with red rags. No – white linen rags red with blood.

It's perfectly normal! she shouted to herself above the noise of the storm that was gathering in her mind.

A monthly bleed is what God intended for a woman.

But her words were drowned out by the winds of time howling in her head, and she staggered to her own room, collapsing on her bed just as the visions swept away all sense of time and place.

Warp:

Monday 17th August 1696

I'm down by the river, up to my elbows in cold water and soap, but the stains are stubborn and no matter how hard I try, I can't get my linen underclothes pure white again. It's early in the morning, but I can't hear the sweet singing of song birds, just the ugly cries of the ravens circling my house, calling my secret out to the wide, wide world. The wind is whispering it through the trees, rustling my shame through the grass right down to the river where I'm sobbing salt tears into the fresh water.

Last night my linen was red and my girlhood was gone, and in the hollow it left behind, a nameless dread crept in and took root. I saw the stains by the light of a candle as I crouched over my chamber pot in the dark, and such a horror fixed hold of my mind that I found myself running from the house out into the night.

Where I ran to I have no idea, but my feet were black with mud when I came to my senses in the morning, and the bloom on my petticoat had blossomed into a scarlet flower. A sudden fear of what I'd done in those lost hours caught hold of my heart, and the blank space in my mind was filled with the sound of a baby's wail – or was it the cawing of a bird?

I mustn't let anyone see my disgrace, else they'll know I'm a woman and ready for the things in the dark and the raven woman even though I'm only eleven and my red, red rags are stuffed between my legs instead of tied to the end of my bed. So I scrub and scrub by the banks of the river till my hands are red and my petticoat's pink and the only white thing left in the whole world is the single cloud that's sailing across the dawn sky. I want to catch at its tails and hold on so it will carry me away up to heaven, but it's leaving me behind just like my girlhood now my time of dreaming and innocence is gone.

"What are you doing?" a voice says in the sudden stillness between the ravens' treacherous cries and the wind's soft betrayal.

I jump and look round, and I see red, red hair framing knowing eyes that have seen too much. Katherine Campbell has come creeping and sneaking through the sunrise and now she's found me out and heard my shame proclaimed in a silent shout on the banks of the river. Those eyes take in the pink stains on my soap-scrubbed petticoat and she laughs a nasty laugh like I'll never have power over her ever again even though I'm the Laird's daughter and she's only a dirty Highlander with a wicked tongue.

"You're a woman now, Christian Shaw," she says, "even though your time's come early. No sense in hiding it – let's go tell your mother the news. She's got little ones enough to fetch and carry for without you pretending you're still one of them."

I cry and clutch at her skirts, but she's skipping off through the field like the early bird who's caught the worm and outwitted the cat and taken its cream for good measure. I go after her, but the rags between my legs slow me down as I'm a woman now and I can't run like the child I used to be.

"Katherine, please!" I call, "let's keep it our secret! I'll give you my best plaid if you'll only hold your tongue!"

"What would I want with your plaid, Mistress Shaw?" she laughs back over her shoulder. "Sure I've got sweethearts enough to buy me ten plaids finer than yours if I only ask them."

We're nearing the courtyard, and soon my secret will be out and everyone will know that my linen is red instead of white and my shame will burn me up from the inside out. I'm trembling and desperate and so, so afraid I can see black spots dancing in front of my eyes where the bright sun's meant to be.

"My silver brooch!" I cry. "Take my silver brooch!

Only don't tell, Katherine, please don't tell."

Katherine stops at the gate and turns to look at me, and for a moment my heart leaps in hope and I think she's taken pity on me. But her eyes are hard and her words are sharp and she tells me I'm a woman now, and women mustn't cry unless they're on the birthing bed with the red rag and the raven women waiting for the bundle of meat to arrive.

Her words become muddled in my head and I don't think I've heard her right, as the ravens are cawing overhead and the blood is pounding in my ears so hard it hurts.

"Christian, what are you doing out there?" says the next voice I hear, and my heart is hammering too when I see it's Mama holding the meaty bundle that turned into baby Jean. She's taking the air and getting the sun on her face, but she's still poorly and I can see the yellow rings around her eyes as she rocks my sister wearily in her arms.

Katherine opens her mouth, but I get there first as there's no red rags round my tongue to slow it down. "I saw Katherine stealing milk!" I blurt out the first thing that flashes into my head. "She was in the cowshed drinking straight from the urn that was meant for the breakfast table."

I know it's a lie, but then it's not, as I imagine her red lips sipping the white liquid so clearly in my mind that it must be the truth.

“That’s a wicked falsehood!” Katherine cries, the tables turned and the fear on her now. “She’s lying! I never did such a thing, Lady Shaw!”

“Katherine Campbell, keep a civil tongue in your head!” Mama snaps, indignant on my behalf but so full of sleep on account of the baby she hardly knows what day of the week it is. “If it happens again, I’ll have you turned out of the house without your month’s pay as punishment, is that clear?”

“But...” Katherine is trying to tell her my secret, but Mama’s tired and tetchy and the baby is wailing and between the three of them no one can be heard but the ravens watching from the windowsills above. Mama goes back into the house and I make sure to drive my victory home the way Papa said that glorious battles are won.

“You keep your mouth shut,” I snarl at Katherine, so low and fierce I’m half dog now instead of half woman. “If you breathe a word to a living soul, I’ll have you accused of so much theft you’ll be swinging from the gallows instead of marching out the front gate without your pay.”

The cook who’s plucking a chicken on the kitchen step and the maid coming from the henhouse with our morning eggs don’t hear me, but the whole world hears the wicked words that Katherine hurls back at me.

"Curse you, Christian Shaw," she spits. "The devil drag your soul through hell for your falsehood!"

I should shiver and shrink from her blasphemy, but I find myself meeting her gaze with a scornful smile instead. She whispered secrets in my ear in the dark and opened my eyes, and I know her curse can't touch me, as I'm a woman now, so I'm already damned.

Weft:

Monday 4th June 1722

"You were missed at supper, Mistress Shaw," Meg said, handing over the mug of hot milk she'd brought upstairs.

I doubt that, Christian thought. Even with Elizabeth souring every one of Jean's excited remarks about Alexander Murray's coming visit with a snide comment, she knew the meal would be a much more relaxed affair without her own oppressive presence.

"And you haven't touched your food!" Meg gazed in dismay at the plate of stew that was still sitting on the tray by the fireplace where she'd left it an hour ago. "Won't you even have some bread and butter before bed?"

"Thank you, Meg, but I'm not hungry," Christian said without looking up. She'd managed to pick herself up from the floor after her dizzy spell earlier before Meg found her in such a weakened state, but she couldn't help asking for the fire to be lit despite the warm June weather. She'd spent the evening hunched in a chair in her room, staring into its depths and cursing herself for letting her feet carry her to the Gallow Green the other day.

I should never have gone there again, she berated herself. *I should have left the past well alone.* Instead, she'd gone and stirred the witches' cauldron full of decomposing memories, and now they were bubbling over the edges of her mind and frothing her waking hours into a frenzy of disturbed thoughts. She'd broken her own rules and given in to the temptation of a warming fire – something her usually iron will managed to refrain from even in the depths of winter. It was a lapse of judgement she now realised would cost her more than just her precious sleep tonight.

The flames flickered orange and yellow, but at their heart they glowed red like the stain on Christian's soul. Their heat burned strangely cold as her mind took her once again down the path to the Gallow Green.

The flames had been red that day in June too. The screams of the condemned had finally stopped, silenced by the executioner's rope, but the horror had only just begun. Christian shivered as she remembered the way the crowd had roared in approval when the pyres had been lit. She had turned to run when the tongues of fire began to lick the soles of the corpses' feet, but her father's iron hand had clamped down on her wrist, forcing her to stay. After everything the family had been through over the previous ten months, he was determined she should see the saga she had started through to the bitter end. Then, as now, Meg had been her only comfort, holding her up when her knees buckled at the sight of so much burning flesh.

"There, mistress," Meg had soothed, *"it's done. They can't hurt you no more."*

Christian had watched as the flames climbed all the way to Katherine Campbell's head. Her mane of red hair had been shaved off in prison, but even in death her lip was curled in a mocking smile. *'I know what you've done, Christian Shaw,'* she seemed to say. *'And your secret will never be safe with me.'* In the blazing heat her eyes popped and melted down her charred face, martyr's tears mixed with taunting laughter.

Christian had clutched Meg's arm tighter, clinging to the one person she could be sure would keep her secrets safe even in death. Her first bleed had stopped abruptly when she took to her sickbed, becoming mixed up in Christian's head with Katherine's bitter curse and her own long illness. She could only hope with the death of the witches who'd caused her misfortunes, they would never return and she'd be free.

The other witches burned one by one: Margaret Lang, the midwife with her red rag and hooked nose that looked so much like a bird's beak by candlelight; Agnes Naismith, the old beggar woman who had called the curse of the raven down on Christian before the executioner's rope had strangled her scream; Maggie Fulton, John Lindsay of Barloch, and brothers John and James Lindsay of Erskine, whose crimes Christian struggled to remember as the flames devoured their features until she could no longer tell which corpse was which.

Her father had finished the long prayer he'd been intoning, pronouncing the *'Amen'* with satisfaction. *"You're free now, Christian,"* he'd told her. *"We're all free of the scourge of witches."*

Christian had choked on the smell of charred flesh, watching the human smoke curling to the sky and wondering if, after this day of horror, she'd feel truly free ever again. And in the sky high above the pyres the ravens had circled, waiting for the feast of flesh that was soon to be served to them.

"You're not sickening for something, are you, mistress?"

Meg's alarmed voice brought Christian back to the present with a start, and she looked up to see the concern in her faithful servant's eyes. Meg remembered only too well the last time her mistress had been ill. At eighteen, Meg had worshipped the eleven-year-old Laird's daughter – half in awe of her cleverness, and half bought by the treats that Christian plied her with to keep her favourite servant fawning over her night and day. It had been only too easy to enlist her help to hide her shameful secret from her mother that August, and to persuade her to act as an accessory to the show that was needed to convince the world that she was bewitched by Katherine Campbell and the rest during that awful time.

I did what was necessary, Christian told herself, gagging on the warm milk that was threatening to come back up at the memory. *I had to rid the town of their evil, no matter the cost.*

The coals popped on the fire, reminding Christian of the way Katherine Campbell used to snap her fingers in derision whenever the other servants said anything she disagreed with. The flames danced like the young woman's red hair on a windy day, and for moment, Christian thought she caught a glimpse of the Highlander's eyes flashing in anger as they hurled the fateful curse at the Laird's daughter all those years ago.

"Mistress Shaw?" Meg's eyes held none of the fire that Katherine's had. They were soft and trusting, only losing their bovine docility when her mistress was slighted or maligned by the gossiping tongues of the townsfolk.

"I'm fine, Meg. Just a little cold. Fetch me my green plaid, will you? There's a chill in the air tonight."

Grateful for the chance to show her devotion, Meg hurried to the chest by the wall, unfolding the long tartans that were stored there. In the firelight Christian could see their coloured threads tinged with a yellow glow. Setting aside Christian's best blue plaid, Meg delved deeper, searching for the warm green plaid she knew her mistress favoured on cooler nights. "Ah, here it is. I'll just... Oh!" Meg realised too late she'd pulled up two plaids instead of one. Hidden below the green plaid, the long red tartan Christian's husband had given her as a wedding gift fell to the floor.

Meg darted a worried look at Christian before snatching it up and stuffing it into the chest again and slamming the lid down. She was privy to nearly all of her mistress's secrets. She knew how much Christian hated the colour red, even though her monthly bleed had never returned after her strange illness as a child.

"Bring it here, Meg," Christian said quickly, trying to pretend she hadn't felt sick at the sight of the red tartan and the marriage it had represented. Katherine Campbell's mocking voice seemed to whisper in her head as Meg crossed the squeaking floorboards, her words full of sinister knowledge.

'Scarlet rags and raven women, and the terrible things men and women do in the dark,' they hissed, as the coals popped and sizzled on the fire. Christian forced herself to smile at Meg despite her mouth watering with the urge to vomit. "You can take that tray down, I'll finish the milk and then turn in for the

night. No, you don't need to stay, I'm perfectly fine."

Christian felt her lips ache with the effort to hold her contented expression right up until the moment Meg closed the bedroom door behind her. As her footsteps faded down the hall, the wind seemed to sigh in relief, breathing down the chimney to stir the flames of the fire to new heights. When Christian moved her chair back to escape the sudden heat, she caught sight of the reflection of the flames in the window. Meg had forgotten to draw the curtains, and in the glow on the glass panes, she saw black shapes writhing in the fire.

Christian leapt to her feet, the green plaid slipping from her shoulders to the floor. Turning back to the fireplace, she saw nothing but coals shifting and settling in the hearth. But there was something moving in the reflected fire on the window. Something dark as coals – sinister, but familiar.

With a pounding heart, Christian crossed the room and looked through the reflected gleam of orange and yellow firelight. Out on the windowsill, framed in the amber sunset that mirrored the hearth's glow, stood two black ravens. At her approach one twisted its neck and fluttered its wings, a strange, wriggling movement that reminded Christian of bodies jerking as the executioner's rope tightened. The other raven leaned forward, striking the window with its powerful beak.

Tap. Tap. Tap. Tap.

Cocking its head, it fixed its black eyes on Christian, the firelight reflected in its penetrating stare.

Christian's breath caught in her throat, her whole body trembling. "What are you trying to tell me?" she whispered, her mouth too dry to add, *'And why now, after twenty-five years?'*

The raven pecked at the window again, louder this time.

Tap. Tap. TAP. TAP.

Christian snatched at the curtains, shutting out the uncanny birds, but the tapping continued, louder and louder until she thought her head would burst. It was only when the light of sunset was blocked and the room was plunged into shadow that she realised the raven's beak wasn't rapping a message. It was pointing to something directly behind her.

She whirled round, searching the shadows for the source of the raven's warning. By the far wall, the chest stood open, the wedding plaid unfurled and lying on the floor. In the firelight, its red threads gleamed, inviting her to remember. It was as though there was a knot tied somewhere in her mind, binding up a bundle of memories that had grown ragged with age. The edges of the knot were fraying, and once again, her mind was unravelling.

The ravens outside her window let loose a terrible cry, and in the depths of her troubled subconscious, she seemed to hear the wail of an infant again. Except this time, it was not the death cry of one baby she could hear.

It was two.

Warp:

Friday 21st August 1696

There's a red cord wrapped around my wrist, and I don't know how it got there. It's one of the curtain ties from my room, but why I'm carrying it like a weapon, and how my feet got so muddy like I've been running through the forest in the depths of night, I have no idea. All I know is that it's sunrise and I'm down by the river again, washing my red linen pink and wishing my world was white instead of shades of shame.

The ravens are circling overhead, and their cries sound like the wails of infants strangled in the crib. I don't know why I think that either. It's a sudden shudder that comes over me, like a half-remembered nightmare broken into fragments by the birds' sharp beaks. I don't remember where I was last night, and that scares me almost as much as the red blood that's washing over the causeway stones.

The sun is rising and the day is creeping forward the way I creep through the fields back to the house before the farmers come out and spot me with my dripping bundle. I feel like I'm Eve running through the garden of Eden to escape the knowledge of her disgrace, but I'm not naked, I'm stuffed full of red rags, and it's not a snake that's chasing me but the ravens that sound like crying bundles of meat pushed down the tunnel of sin under cover of night.

I freeze at the gate to the courtyard.

Someone is standing by the well talking to my sister Elizabeth. Lizzie's only six and still a little girl, and she's standing there in her nightshirt rubbing her eyes like she's just got out of bed and come looking for me. There are eyes all around me – eyes in the windows where the ravens are perched on the sills and on the rooftops where they peer down with black mirrors that pierce my soul. The stranger turns, and now her red-rimmed eyes are on me too, searching out the secret shame I'm hiding behind my back.

"Greetings, Mistress Shaw," the old woman says, half-curtseying on creaking legs as I'm the Laird's eldest daughter and I command respect. "How are you this fine morning?"

It's Agnes Naismith come begging again at our kitchen door, and she's caught me out with my secrets in one hand and my disgrace staining the back of my nightdress. If I turn around she'll discover them both, so I edge along the wall to the kitchen door so only the ravens high above can see.

"Mistress Shaw, are you quite well?" Agnes Naismith's eyes are red and rheumy, but she can see clear through me like I'm made of glass. I almost shatter under her hungry stare as she takes in my mud-covered feet, my nightdress damp with morning dew, and the strange red cord that's wrapped around my wrist like a hangman's noose on execution day. She's slow and simple and doesn't know her letters from a child's scratchings in the dirt, but I know she's full of women's knowledge just like Katherine Campbell, and she can read the signs of original sin carved into my flesh like I'm a living book of Genesis. I'm feeling faint so I can't work out what she's thinking when her eyes travel up to my face, but she's just an old beggar woman and I'm the Laird's daughter, so I conjure an image of her exulting at her power over me, and my stomach lurches like I'm going to be sick.

"It must be the babe keeping you up at night and making you so pale," she says, the words oozing from her wrinkled lips like pulp from a rotting plum. I shudder to think of the clock that's ticking away inside me, slowly decaying my flesh now that I'm a woman too and turning me little by little into this walking horror of melted flesh under withered skin.

Agnes is talking again, but I'm struggling to hear her words above the cawing of ravens that sounds like the wailing of infants, and the red cord is tightening around my wrist like it's trying to warn me I've done something terrible I mustn't forget.

"Are your mother and the babe any better?" she asks through her rotting plum lips. "I hear they've been poorly recently. You will give them my best wishes for their health, won't you?"

She's saying nice things to buy herself the oatbread and milk she wants from our kitchen, but the cook isn't out yet and the maid is still in the cowshed, so she says her oversweet words to me instead. I try to nod, but my head is leaden and I sway, the wet bundle heavy in my hands behind my back. Lizzie's plucking at my arm asking where I've been and why I'm all muddy and wailing that she wants to go back to bed, but I'm scared to move as I can feel the rags between my legs grow slick with fresh blood, and there's a sticky stream running down one thigh beneath my nightdress. My feet are frozen in fear at the thought of this stranger and my innocent little sister learning my terrible secrets, but my mind is racing, racing, racing till at last it reaches a safe haven.

Meg.

I need to tell Meg. She who hugs me before bed and brings me hot milk on cold nights and never has a cross word for me even when I make extra work for her. Her eyes aren't knowing like Katherine Campbell's or red-rimmed like Agnes Naismith's. Meg's eyes are gentle and obedient just like a servant's should be, and too dull to reflect any of the secrets that might be hidden behind them. If I can just get back to the house to tell Meg, then everything will be alright.

But Lizzie's hanging on my arm, my wet bundle's weighing me down, the shame is running red between my legs, and Agnes Naismith is standing between me and the door to safety. The old woman wants her breakfast, and maybe she's worked out that secrets will buy her food faster than sweet words, for her red eyes grow keen as she looks me up and down and asks after my health again and then how old I am.

She knows she knows she knows!

She knows I'm a woman now and not a girl, and just like Katherine Campbell she'll have power over me if I don't find a way to snatch it back quick. I can see the kitchen maid coming out of the cowshed with the pail of breakfast milk, and I open my mouth to make an accusation that'll turn the tables on the old woman who's sniffing out my secrets.

But justthen the early morning wind blows sharper round the courtyard, and Agnes Naismith draws her shawl up over her bony shoulders where the flesh has melted away. That's when I see it. I see the patchwork pieces that make up her tattered plaid, and one of the tartan squares is red, red, red like the blood on my thighs and the cord around my wrist. For a moment, just a moment, I catch a glimpse of a tiny face in a crib growing redder and redder as a curtain tie wraps tighter around its neck in the night, but then my vision dims again and all that's left is the memory of crimson and the cries of the ravens on the rooftops.

"Mistress Shaw, are you quite well?" It's Kitty, the kitchen maid, who's asking this time, putting down her pail and pushing Agnes Naismith out of the way like the old woman has no more worth than a stone on the road. The old woman stumbles into Lizzie, and somehow they manage to overturn the milk pail, because suddenly there's white all over the grey stones and Kitty is shouting at Agnes Naismith and Lizzie is howling and the ravens are crying, crying, crying up above.

If I don't move now my secrets will be shown to the world, so I shuffle to the kitchen door with my back and my bundle to the wall, and shove my way inside before the red on my thighs can stain the front of my nightdress. The cook doesn't see as she's leaning over the hearth lighting the kitchen fire and I run, run, run all the way upstairs to my room where I can hide my bundle and my shame in the chamber pot and wait for Meg to come and save me from my sins.

Weft:

Wednesday 6th June 1722

The afternoon sun shimmered on the barrels of buttermilk lined up in the courtyard – the finest the cows on the Bargarran estate could produce. Christian knew her mother and sisters thought it was a terrible waste using such a precious resource on her bleaching experiments, but from her fact-finding trip to Holland, she also knew how essential it was to the whitening process.

The servants eyed her nervously as she paced up and down the courtyard, monitoring their work and issuing instructions as though she were a drill sergeant at the army barracks.

"Make sure the skeins are fully immersed, Janet, it's no good if they're just floating on the surface."

"Don't stir the milk so vigorously, Bess, you'll get the thread all tangled up."

"How many times do I have to tell you to roll your sleeves up, John? You'll pollute the milk if that dirty smock gets anywhere near it."

Christian could see the resentment behind the eyes that were lowered every time she leaned over a milk barrel and voiced her disapproval, but she knew if she didn't tightly control every stage of the process, she'd never get the results she so badly wanted. Her thread had to be white as new snowfall. White as starlight. White as the innocence she desperately tried to cling to despite the haunting visions that had been troubling her ever since she'd made the mistake of visiting the witches' execution grounds on the Gallow Green.

"Are you sure those skeins were washed properly with white soap this morning, Bess?" she frowned, eyeing the long threads she'd laboured many days to spin. "They still look too yellow."

"I scrubbed them for a full three hours, Widow Millar," the servant replied, showing Christian her hands that were pink and chapped from a whole morning spent up to her elbows in soapy water. "They're as white as can be already, and they haven't been soaked and sunned yet. The good Lord himself couldn't make lilies any whiter than these threads." She was trying hard to keep the exasperation from her voice, but all of the servants were losing patience with Christian's endless demands to make the thread whiter, whiter, whiter.

There's something missing from the bleaching process, Christian thought to herself in frustration. *Some vital step I haven't found yet.*

The cawing of ravens on the rooftops seemed to be mocking her, and she glanced up to see two sitting on the windowsill of the library where one of her bleaching slates was fixed. She couldn't be sure, but she had an uneasy feeling they were the same birds who'd been sitting outside her bedroom the previous night. As one opened its beak and let loose a mocking cry, her eyes came to rest on the threads fixed to the slate behind the glass pane. Christian gasped, her whole body stiffening in shock. Where once there had been a row of pale white threads, the skeins bleaching in the sunlight were mottled red, the colour of dried meat on a butcher's slab.

That can't be right! Christian thought, her head reeling. *I checked the test slate just this morning and the threads were the whitest they've been yet!*

Perhaps it was too many hours spent hunched over her spinning wheel, straining her eyesight in the evenings, or too little exercise outdoors that was affecting her vision. Or perhaps it was simply the afternoon sun glancing off the windowpanes that was playing tricks on her tired mind. She turned to ask Bess what colour she thought the skeins in the library windows were, and her heart nearly stopped in fright. The milk in the servant's barrel was blood red, churning with each twist of the stirring pole like some unholy devil's brew.

Christian staggered back, her hands flying to her face to shield her eyes from the terrible sight. *No, no, no!* a young girl's voice wailed in her head. *It's happening again! Please make it stop.*

"Widow Millar? Are you quite well?" The note of concern in Janet's voice brought her back to her senses faster than a doctor's tonic. She mustn't be seen to be weak. She mustn't be suspected of any frailty. Not now when her family needed her to be strong and build the business that was their only hope of escaping from financial ruin.

"I'm fine, Janet, just a little hot," she said, forcing her voice to remain steady. Pretending to have raised her hands to wipe sweat from her brow in the late afternoon glare, she hid her shudder of relief when she saw that the barrel of milk was indeed creamy white, and not blood red after all. A quick glance up at the windows confirmed her suspicions. The skeins bleaching there were pale white, not marbled like fatty flesh. The ravens on the windowsill cawed louder as though mocking her momentary lapse, and Christian clenched her fists, determined not to let superstition and childish delusions from the past get the better of her.

"Make sure you secure the lids on those barrels firmly," she snapped at the servants, doubling down on her demands. "I don't want that buttermilk touched for the next four days. If so much as a single skein comes out less white than the last batch, I'll dock your wages for shoddy work, is that clear?"

The servants muttered their resentful assent, leaving Christian in no doubt that her reputation was intact. ignoring the jeers of the ravens on the rooftops, she marched back into the house, escaping to her room to apply a cooling compress to her forehead and gather her tangled thoughts.

Her respite didn't last long. She'd just sent Meg down to help in the kitchen after smartening her mistress up for supper, when she heard the bustle in the hall which signalled the arrival of their important guest. She hurried out to intercept Elizabeth at the top of the stairs, determined to ensure this evening would be a success for her youngest sister's sake.

"You'll remember to mind your manners, Elizabeth, won't you?" Christian urged, catching at her arm before she descended. "Make sure not to say anything unpleasant that might offend Master Murray."

"Me?" Elizabeth shook her sister's hand off with a snort of derision. "If the great Alexander Murray chooses not to ally himself with this family after we've gone and slaughtered a calf and half our henhouse on his behalf, it won't be my doing. You're the one who's stopped this family prospering all these years, Christian, not me."

"Elizabeth, that isn't fair." Christian felt the words cut all the more deep for their truth, despite her protests. "I've laboured all the hours God grants me to return this family to its rightful position in society."

"Yes, but what have you been doing with all the hours the devil grants you, dear sister, answer me that?" Elizabeth sneered. It was her idea of a joke – she had no idea that her words filled Christian's heart full of horror.

"Elizabeth! You surely don't suspect that I'm a...? After everything I went through during the trials, you can't still have any doubt that I'm anything but a devout—"

"Lord, it's been twenty-five years! Can't you take a jest even now?" Elizabeth rolled her eyes. "If you really were a witch, your tongue would have shrivelled up and dropped off an age ago with all the prayers you spout. Don't think I can't hear you through the walls at night – I'd rather you were in league with the devil if it meant I got a good night's sleep without all of that racket."

"Elizabeth!" Christian's jaw dropped at her sister's blasphemy, but Elizabeth just gave an amused snort and stomped down the staircase.

The malicious edge to her sister's high spirits did not bode well for the success of the evening's entertainment. Muttering a quick prayer, Christian hurried after her, determined to do her very best to keep Elizabeth and her wicked tongue away from Alexander Murray.

The guests had already gathered in the dining room when Christian joined them. Despite the warmth of the evening, a fire had been lit to highlight the richly carved mantle and show the room to its best advantage, and Christian felt stifled from the moment she crossed the threshold.

"Ah! Widow Millar, there you are. It's a pleasure to see you again after such a long absence." A sumptuously dressed gentleman stepped forward, the lace on his cuffs flapping around his manicured hands as he gave a flourishing bow. Christian shot Elizabeth a look to silence her snigger and gave a simple nod in return.

"I'm pleased to see you've come back from your travels safe and well, Master Murray," she replied. "And is this your sister, Isabella?" She smiled politely at the younger woman who was dressed almost as gaudily as her brother. "It's been such a long time since we met, I almost didn't recognise you."

She'd meant it as a pleasant greeting, but from the way the young woman's eyes narrowed in contempt, Christian could tell she'd taken it as a slight.

"Yes, it's been years. In fact, I don't think we've met since we were children. Not since your strange 'illness' that had us all so worried."

Christian could see her mother's face go pale in the

fire's orange glow, and Lady Shaw's mouth flapped up and down like a drowning fish as she floundered for something to say to smooth over the awkward moment. Before Christian could think of a courteous reply, her youngest sister got there first. "This is Isabella's husband, Charles McNab," Jean said quickly, gesturing to the young man who stood looking haughtily out of the window as though sizing up the value of their land.

"And this is Isabella's brother-in-law, Robert McNab."

The corpulent youth tore his eyes from the dishes being set on the dinner table for a brief moment to flash Christian a fleeting smile.

"It's a pleasure to make your acquaintance," Christian said, mentally adding the lie to the list of sins she'd pray to have forgiven before she went to bed. "And did you all accompany Master Murray on his Grand Tour of Europe?"

A single snort was all the reply she got from the disdainful young man at the window, and Christian wasn't sure if it was aimed at her or at the thought of spending any more time with the foppish Alexander Murray than he had to for this wife's sake. His younger brother was more forthcoming, using her question as a distraction from the torture of watching the servants lay out the steaming dishes he hadn't been invited to taste yet.

"Oh, good Lord, no! All of that jolting about in uncomfortable carriages on endless roads and eating goodness knows what in foreign countries for months on end? Not for me, Widow Millar, no, no! And my brother and his wife have more sense than that too, thankfully. But can't you tell that Alexander's the only one who's been to France?"

Christian looked at the simpering gentleman again, trying to think of a polite way of saying that it certainly looked like his wardrobe was even more pretentious than the last time they had met. "Well... You do look a little more tanned, Master Murray. It seems the French climate has agreed with you."

Alexander Murray guffawed as though she'd said something outrageously funny, and the younger McNab joined in, his chubby chest heaving with mirth. "No, no, that's not it at all, Widow Millar," Robert McNab chortled. "Haven't you noticed? Don't you know the custom for visitors to France? The French have these silly rules, you see. The wearing of red shoes is restricted to men of courtly status. So what do you think the fashion is for young hinds like Murray here to show they've been on the Grand Tour? Go on, show her, Alex."

Alexander Murray gave another flourishing bow, this time pointing to his feet. Christian looked down to see he was wearing a pair of crimson high-heeled shoes, tied at the arches with matching red ribbon. She opened her mouth to voice her polite admiration, but found that nothing came out except a croak that echoed round the room like the startled cry of a raven.

"I beg your pardon?" Alexander Murray glanced up quizzically, still waiting for his compliment.

"I— I—" Christian stammered, but her voice ended in another croak, this one more desperate than the first.

The red ties on his feet are a red cord round my wrist that squeezed and squeezed until the bundle of meat stopped wailing and the raven woman's work was all undone. The high-pitched voice of a terrified child danced round and round her head until she was dizzy trying to catch its meaning.

"Widow Millar, are you ill?" Isabella frowned, stepping back as though afraid she'd already been contaminated merely by being in the same room as someone with such an infamous history.

"I'm perfectly fine," Christian managed to gasp out. "I've been outside all day and am a little hot and fatigued, that's all. It's the fire, and the heat in here, and... Excuse me, everyone, I think I just need to lie down for an hour. Jean, would you send Meg up to me, please?"

Christian tried to hold her head high as she left the room, but as soon as she reached the stairs the effort became too much and she clutched at the banisters, the hallway spinning around her. Meg came hurrying from the kitchen at the summons, taking hold of her mistress's arm and spiriting her up the stairs before anyone could see her in such a weakened state. She knew how important it was for Christian to keep up appearances. She knew almost everything about her past, and Christian could trust her with almost every one of her secrets.

Almost.

"You rest there, Mistress Shaw," she soothed, settling Christian down on the bed with her gentle hands and making sure she was comfortable. "You've overworked yourself these last few weeks with your spinning and bleaching, and you need to give yourself a break from it."

Christian let her maid fuss over her, enjoying the attention for once. It reminded her of when she was a very young child, before her sisters came along and she was the only daughter. Her brothers had quickly learned to shun their mother's kisses and bedtime stories as 'unmanly', and for a few happy years before Elizabeth appeared, Christian had her mother's attention all to herself. It was bad enough when there was just one sister to compete with, but after Jean came along it was as if Christian didn't exist.

My illness changed all that, Christian thought woozily, her head feeling heavy and muddled as Meg blew out the candle and tiptoed out, leaving the room in soft shadow. *I was the most important person in this house for nearly a full year.*

As she drifted off to sleep, the memory of her mother's mild eyes gazed down at her from the shadows by her bedside, filled only with concern, and not with the fear that came later.

Warp:

Monday 24th August 1696

Mama's fingers are soft as feathers as they flutter at my forehead, soothing the fever that's taken hold of my churning, burning mind. Papa's standing over my bed too, and he's looking at me – really, *really* looking – in a way he hasn't done since I was Elizabeth's age when he'd let me sit on his knee by the fire after supper. My body is aching and my thoughts are spiralling like water down the waste gutter, but I don't want to get better ever again if this sickness keeps my parents by my bedside with tender hands and loving eyes.

"How can this have happened so suddenly?" I can hear Mama saying like she's far, far away and her voice is echoing down a long, dark hallway even though she's sitting on the bed with my head in her lap. "She was fine until Saturday morning when Meg found her having a fit in her sleep."

I want to stretch out my arms and kiss my faithful Meg for hiding all my secrets and risking her eternal soul by lying to cover my sins, but she's standing at the far end of the bed folding linen and I can't reach her as my body's twitching and jerking like my mattress is lined with the coals of hell.

I did something bad, bad, bad on Friday night, and when I woke at dawn in the courtyard with the red cord round my wrist again and my soaking rags staining my nightdress, I remembered, just for a moment, what I'd done. I remembered where I'd been last Sunday night, and Thursday night too, and the things I did then to unravel the raven woman's work. It was like an unholy light filled my head in a sudden flash, and for the briefest of instants I understood why the cries of the ravens up above me sounded so like the wailing of meaty bundles pushed down the tunnels of sin in the dark. I fell down in a fit right there and then, and if it hadn't been for Meg coming out early to find me and carrying me to my room, my secrets would be out by now. She washed me and changed my linen before calling my parents, and now my shame has dried up and there's no more red, there's just the sweet bliss of childish innocence once more, and the fond looks and caresses of my parents that I never want to lose again.

I don't remember now what I did, and I'm never going to remember again. I've buried the memories deep, deep down where no one can find them, but I'm still scared that Katherine Campbell with her knowing woman's smile and Agnes Naismith with her hungry, red-rimmed eyes will spy them out. Every time I shut my eyes to rest I see them looking back at me, and the fear of discovery is twisting my body into knots as I lie in my bed and pray, pray, pray for forgiveness.

"John White couldn't work out what's wrong with her, and my cousin has read more books on medicine than any man I know outside the profession," I hear Papa say from a long way off in the distance. "I've sent for Doctor Johnstone in Paisley. He should be here any minute."

Doctor.

That word holds no terror for me now. My bleeding has stopped before I was found out, and a man isn't going to guess my secrets the way the knowing eyes of women like Katherine Campbell and Agnes Naismith can. Let him come. Maybe he'll have a cure for the hellfire that's scorching my skin and burning me up from the inside out all at once.

I must have fallen asleep, as next thing I know the room is darker and the doctor's leaning over me with his stale breath and beefy hands, and I'm squirming, squirming, squirming under his clammy touch like he's the raven woman and I'm the meaty bundle coming down the tunnel of sin with a high-pitched wail.

"I need to drain the ill humours," the stale beef man says, opening his bag and pulling out little metal things that glitter ominously in the candlelight. "That will relieve the tension and clear the blockage to return the circulation to normal."

The stale beef man speaks more nonsense words that don't frighten me right up until the point he pulls a cord out of his bag. It's red, red, red as the one I carried round my wrist like a weapon, and before I can jerk my arm free he's tied it round my elbow and bitten into my arm with tiny metal jaws.

Everything goes dark, and for a time I'm not a girl in bed but a raven with soot-stained feathers flying through the black, black night on wings of death. Then I'm falling out of the sky, crashing to the ground and breaking my wings into a thousand pieces, and I'm no longer cloaked in midnight black but stained red with crimson shame for all the world to see.

I open my eyes and look down, and find my nightmare's come true. It's not my wing that's torn open but my arm – the red cord's squeezing tight and there's a steady stream of scarlet trickling down my arm into the bowl the stale beef man is holding. I lurch upright with a gasp, and there in the pool of red, red, blood I can see the sin in my eyes reflected back at me by candlelight.

That's when I start screaming.

My shrieks are so loud they scare the ravens from the rooftops where they've been roosting, and they go flying into the midnight sky with the cries of strangled babes. My body's possessed by fear and I can no more control it than I can control the terrible images that are racing through my head. It's like the light's gone out in my mind and all that's left are shadows looming larger in the pale glow of guttering candles. I can see the raven woman's beak nose and scissoring fingers flickering on the walls of my remembrance, and Katherine Campbell's running through my memory, trying to reach Mama in the courtyard before me to tell her of my shame. In the darkness before dawn, Agnes Naismith is dancing, dancing, dancing through my bad dreams with her red tartan shawl held high and her red-rimmed eyes devouring my secrets for breakfast.

I scream their names over and over and over until my throat is raw and I'm croaking the way the ravens do at dusk. Mama is crying in fear and Papa is pacing up and down shouting at the stale beef man to do something, but Meg, my gentle Meg, is holding me, rocking me, soothing me until it's over and I'm all wrung out like the dirty red rags I washed pink in the river.

In the calm after the storm, the voices in my room are full of foreboding as they whisper round my bed.

"This isn't natural, is it, Doctor?" Papa's voice is strained to breaking point.

"I've never seen anything quite so extreme," the stale beef man agrees.

"Why would she call those names?" Mama says, sounding more afraid than she's ever been in her life.

For a moment I'm afraid too, even though I'm so tired I barely have the strength to shudder at the thought of my secrets being revealed. But Meg comes to my rescue again, explaining it all away so I can be pure and spotless and innocent again.

"Katherine Campbell laid a curse on the poor child just last Monday, Lady Shaw – do you remember the servants talking of it? She was accused of stealing milk, and instead of owning up to her bad deeds, she called down the devil to drag Mistress Shaw's soul through hell. I heard the words fall from her lips with my own ears"

"That's right!" Mama gasps. "And Lizzie was in such a state on Friday after that old tramp, Agnes Naismith, came begging at the kitchen door. Little Lizzie said she'd put the fear of God into Christian with all her prying questions, and then upset the milk pail out of spite when she didn't get the answers she wanted from her."

"It's a bad business," Papa says heavily, like the weight of the whole world has come to rest on his shoulders and he's struggling to breathe. "I fear this is beyond your expertise, Doctor Johnstone. I need to consult with the presbytery to see what can be done for my daughter."

“You suspect witchcraft, then?” the stale beef man asks, though it doesn’t sound like a question, it sounds like he’s agreeing.

“I do,” Papa says darkly. “I do.”

It's the last thing I hear before my head falls back on my pillow and my aching bones melt into the mattress like I’m no more than a pat of butter left too near the kitchen fire.

Witchcraft! I think woozily. *That’s what it must be.*

It’s not my scarlet shame or the terrible things I did on my own in the dark that’s brought this suffering upon me, it’s the knowing smile of Katherine Campbell, the hungry eyes of Agnes Naismith, and the red rag of the raven woman that’s caused it all. The stale beef man doesn’t know how to end my torment, but Papa does. All I have to do is trust my papa, and my faithful Meg, and everything will be alright, and I’ll never need to hear the screams of dying children from the mouths of ravens ever again.

Weft:

Wednesday 6th June 1722

"Ah, Widow Millar! You're just in time to join us for something sweet to finish your mother's excellent meal." Alexander Murray swayed to his feet with as much ceremony as he could manage in his drunken state to show what a perfect gentleman he was as Christian entered the dining room.

"Are you well rested?" his sister Isabella asked, the look of disdain on her face only becoming more pronounced during the three courses Christian had been absent. "We wouldn't want you to overtax yourself for the sake of a bowl of sponge pudding." She gave the soft cake a withering stare and set down her spoon with a thump.

Outside, the weather seemed to mirror her mood. Despite the afternoon ending in sunshine and the evening starting bright and fair, a storm was gathering, black clouds heavy with rain rolling across the louring sky. The curtains had been drawn, but the wind was whistling through every tiny chink between wood and stone it could find, stirring the thick material and sending the shadows of flickering candles dancing across the walls. The fire crackled restlessly, the flames leaping as though in warning with each pop of unsettled coal.

Christian shivered. When she'd left the room earlier she'd been burning up, but despite the fire glowing hotter and brighter on her return, she couldn't shake the cold chill that now clung to her bones.

"I'm much better, thank you," she lied as she sat down at the end of the table. "A short nap did me the power of good. Don't let me interrupt – please, go on with what you were saying."

The second the words were out of her mouth she regretted them. A quick glance around the table told her the conversation had not been to her family's taste. Her mother's knuckles were white as they clutched her spoon, the rigid smile pasted on her face looking waxen in the candlelight. Elizabeth was trading venomous scowls with Isabella, and Jean's polite laughter was becoming more high-pitched with each sarcastic comment Charles McNab made about his brother-in-law's silly French cuffs dangling in the food. The only person at the table oblivious to the tension was the young Robert McNab, whose eyes were fixed on the bowl he leant over, while his jaws chomped with the feverish intensity of a glutton who was terrified this would be his last meal for a whole ten minutes.

"Master Murray was telling us all about his time in Rome, Christian," Jean said too brightly. "He was saying that he visited the ruins of—"

"Actually, we'd finally moved on from the tedious Tour and my brother was discussing some of the new tenant farmers he's just hired for his estate," Isabella interrupted. There was a nasty gleam in her eye, and Christian had the sinking feeling that somehow the conversation was going to be connected to the past she was so desperate to forget.

"That's right, so I was," Alexander Murray beamed, flush with wine and happy to be the centre of attention again. "One of the young men I've just taken on is James Montgomery. Pretty little wife he has too – she'll keep the cottage nice and clean, not like the old shrew who lives next door. Do you know, last week that old hag had the cheek to—"

"You'll know of James Montgomery, won't you, Widow Millar?" Isabella interrupted, eager to keep the conversation on the topic she suspected would get her the most satisfying reaction.

"No, I can't say that I do," Christian said. "We've kept mostly to ourselves since my father and my brothers passed away, and I haven't kept up with the comings and goings of the farmers outwith our estate."

"Ah, but James Montgomery is a local worker, isn't he,

Alexander?" Isabella prompted.

"Yes – you must have known of his father, surely, Widow Millar? Will— hic! Excuse me..." he burped and took another long gulp of wine. "William Montgomery lived not too far from here when you were a girl," he finished, filling his cup again and getting just as much liquid on the table.

The name sent a shiver of recognition down Christian's spine, and she fought to keep her composure as Isabella added gleefully, "It was a terrible thing that happened to his family, wasn't it, Widow Millar?"

"What happened?" Charles McNab asked, taking an interest in the conversation for the first time. "What was terrible?"

"The way his baby died. You remember it, don't you, Alexander?"

Now he finally had the attention of his contemptuous brother-in-law, Alexander Murray wanted very much to keep it, but the wine had rushed to his head and he was slurring his words. "Yes, no. Yes... What was the question again, Issie?"

Isabella ignored him, taking up the story herself to make sure it had the maximum effect. "I remember the events very clearly. It was right around the time Widow Millar – Mistress Shaw as she was then – first fell ill. We heard that William Montgomery's baby daughter had been strangled in the night."

"Strangled?" Charles McNab leaned forward, his former ennui forgotten, and even his insatiable younger brother put his spoon down for a moment to listen.

"Yes, and she wasn't the only one. There were two other children that died around the same time – Matthew Park's infant daughter, and another local worker's child, were also killed."

Christian's skin prickled with cold despite the heat of the fire. Something about Isabella's words chilled her, as though a shard of ice had pierced her heart. Or maybe it had been there all along. Perhaps it was a long-buried memory that was finally surfacing, cutting her to the quick as it tunnelled its way out of the dark where it had been hidden for so long.

"But surely they just died in their sleep?" Robert McNab blinked, his eyes slightly glazed from the amount of food he'd consumed.

"Ah, unfortunately, no," Isabella sighed theatrically. "They were all found in the morning with tell-tale marks around their necks – sure signs of foul play in the night."

"And did they discover who did such wicked deeds?" Charles McNab asked.

"Not right away, but during the investigation into..." Isabella paused with fake delicacy, shooting Christian a glance to make sure her words were hitting the mark before hurrying on. “Let’s just say that during that unpleasant business with the witches long ago, several of the accused confessed to the crime.”

“But this isn’t the dark ages!” her husband protested. “Surely confession under the conditions of torture the accused were no doubt subjected to was not enough to prove their guilt?”

“Ah, but there were other reasons for suspecting their involvement,” Isabella said with evident relish. “Weren’t there, Widow Millar?”

The room went silent, everyone turning to look at Christian. She could feel the ice spreading from her chest to the very tips of her fingers. Her tongue hung heavy in her mouth, strange images whirling too fast round her mind for her to catch. “I— I—” she stammered, uncharacteristically inarticulate. Her mother’s face was ashen in the candlelight, the mention of her family’s involvement in the witch trials still able to render her speechless with shame and fear even after so many years had passed. Jean’s nervous smile was pulled so tight her lips looked in danger of snapping at any second. It was only Elizabeth, with her burning resentment at her name being dragged through the mud in a business she’d been too young to understand, who kept her head.

“Christian was very sick at the time, she can hardly be expected to remember any of the details about the investigation, can she?" Elizabeth snapped, trying to put an end to the subject. Isabella, smelling the intoxicating scent of secret scandal, was not about to be put off so easily.

"Well, I was the same age, and I remember the details clearly," Isabella sniffed. "Those two brothers, John and James Lindsay, were said to have been the ringleaders. You remember the Lindsay brothers, surely, Widow Millar?" Isabella continued to needle her. "They were notorious witches, everybody said so. I'm just surprised they weren't burned sooner. They were always out in the woods at night – that was the irrefutable evidence that damned them in the end. Secret rituals, the Commission found. Communing with the devil out in the dark." Isabella shivered in sheer delight at the effect her words had on her captive audience.

"They were hunting rabbits," Christian said, her voice coming out no louder than a whisper. "They were hungry and they hunted in the woods at night. They were just hungry..."

"Excuse me, Widow Millar? Did you say something?" Isabella smiled gleefully.

In the silence that followed, the wind howled in the distancc, the unseasonal storm approaching with ferocious speed. Charles McNab glanced towards the shivering curtains warily, and seemed on the point of saying something that might break up the gathering, when his wife interrupted him.

"Then there was that other woman who was accused – the midwife. Margaret Lang, wasn't it? She delivered all of your children, didn't she, Lady Shaw?" Isabella turned her attention to Christian's mother, enjoying the way the older woman squirmed in her seat as through trying desperately to escape from her part in the story.

"I couldn't have known!" Lady Shaw's frightened squeak was barely audible over the boom of thunder as it crashed around the house. "I couldn't have known she was a witch!"

"Isabella, my dear," Charles McNab began, "I think if we don't make a start for home now, the storm might prevent—"

"And who was the other witch accused of strangling the babes?" Isabella continued, paying no attention to her husband and barely noticing the howling of the wind around the house. Her eyes glittered maliciously in the guttering candles' glare, and she turned the full force of her contemptuous scowl on Christian. "I seem to remember the Commission who interviewed witnesses found evidence that the old beggar woman... what was her name, again? Oh, Agnes Naismith – well, she had visited the Montgomery's house just a few weeks before the babe was strangled, asking after the child's health and what age she was. Weren't those the very questions she asked you, the day before you took to your sick bed, Widow Millar?"

Christian's head was pounding, and a wave of nausea threatened to overwhelm her. She knew there was nothing behind Isabella's words except a mean-spirited attempt to show her family in a bad light and convince her brother he'd be throwing himself away if he offered Jean Shaw his hand, but still...

She knows she knows she knows! a child's voice screamed in her head above the rumble of thunder and the wailing of the wind that sounded strangely like the cry of babes strangled in the night. *Katherine Campbell has whispered my secrets in her ear and now she knows all about the red, red cord that undid the raven woman's work in the dark.*

"She was a strange one, that Agnes Naismith," Isabella frowned, trying harder to get a response out of Christian who was frozen in her chair, her eyes unblinking. "I remember the day of the burnings on the Gallow Green – what a sight!"

"Issie, dearest, I don't think this is a terribly ple— hic! pleasant subject for the dinner table." Her brother patted her hand clumsily, noticing at last through his drunken stupor that Jean's bottom lip was trembling and Lady Shaw was pale as death.

Isabella ignored him too, her eyes triumphant as she

drove home the final coffin nail she held to bury Jean's hopes of marrying into the Murray family. "Didn't she curse you, Mistress Millar, with her dying breath?"

"Curse?" Alexander Murray slurred, exchanging glances with the young Robert McNab. Silently, the two of them slid their chairs further back from the women of the Shaw family, as though afraid of catching some invisible contagion.

"Yes, you remember, Alexander," Isabella crowed. "She laid a blood curse on the Shaw family for their falsehood – as she called it – and damned them to hell."

"That's a lie!" Elizabeth slapped her hand down so hard on the table she upset the wine jug. "She shouted out some nonsense words before she was strangled, and that's all. They were the ramblings of a mad woman, that's what they were, nothing more."

But the damage has been done, and Isabella's words had the desired effect. Her brother swayed to his feet, thanking Lady Shaw for a lovely dinner and making his drunken excuses to leave.

"But you can't go home in this weather!" Lady Shaw protested, finding her voice at last. "The storm is too wild. Stay the night – we'll have beds made up for you. It's no trouble at all."

"It's not so bad," Robert McNab said, eager to get away now that the food was gone. "Look, it's barely even—" Just as he drew the curtains, a flash of lightning lit up the sky, rain hammering so hard against the window the glass shuddered in its frame. Everyone jumped, except Christian. It wasn't the lightning that scared her, or the ferocity of the storm.

It was the sight of the ravens sitting on the windowsill staring in at her that nearly stopped her heart with fear.

Before there had been two. Now there were three.

Three little babes all strangled in a row, but the question is: does Isabella know? sang a child's voice in Christian's head as the black eyes peered back at her. In another moment Robert McNab had closed the curtains again, but the singsong voice only got louder, drowning out the other voices in the room as Lady Shaw urged her guests to stay, and the visitors argued amongst themselves about the best plan of action. The discussion was interrupted by Mary the kitchen maid coming back in carrying a tray filled with sweet curdled milk and wine.

"The posset, Lady Shaw," she said, setting the laden tray down on the table. "I've spiced it well with cinnamon and nutmeg to ward off the chill."

"Um, perhaps staying the night might be the best idea after all?" Robert McNab said tentatively, glancing hopefully at the head of his party. Alexander Murray was already sitting back down and reaching for his wine glass. Isabella threw her husband a furious look, but Charles McNab could only shrug and nod at the window, as though the decision had been made by the weather.

As Lady Shaw reached for the steaming pot to serve her guests, Christian's eyes widened in horror as she watched the lid being lifted to reveal the curdled white milk mixed with red wine.

Their necks were white, then red, red, red when the deed was done and we did run, the voice sang, high pitched and gleeful inside her head. The bile rose so fast in her throat she barely had time to cover her mouth with her napkin to catch a mouthful of vomit before the others could notice her discomfort.

"Excuse me, everyone, I think I'll say goodnight now." She forced her legs to support her, clenching her trembling hands into fists. "No, Master Murray, don't get up, I'll leave you all to your posset. I wish you all pleasant dreams."

One step, two steps, three steps... Christian counted them all the way out to the hallway and to the foot of the stairs. The darkness closed around her as she mounted the steps to her room, the child's piping voice singing a sinister lullaby that woke the sleeping memories buried deep in her mind.

Warp:

Saturday 22nd August 1696

It's past the witching hour and well into the pitch black before the turn of morning when my senses come back to me and I find myself running through the forest. The ravens are circling overhead, watching me with their knowing eyes that see all as I stumble down the path and trip over tree roots in the dark. I don't know why I'm here or what I've done, but I can feel the red rags between my legs growing wet and heavy, and the one certain thing in this fog of confusion is that I have to get back home so Meg can wash my shame away before the whole world sees.

The ravens are crying, crying, crying and I can't understand why they sound so much like strangled babes when they should be croaking and cawing instead of piercing my soul with their unnatural wails. Suddenly there's another sound crashing towards me through the densely packed trees, and my heart stands still in horror when I realise the devil has caught up with me at last despite all my desperate prayers, and now he's come to drag me down to hell like Katherine Campbell bid him do.

I fall to my knees and clasp my hands in a useless plea for mercy as a dark shape looms over me with eyes as red as burning coals and a voice that hisses out through glittering fangs. "What are you doing out here, little mistress? It's too late for a young one like you to be here on your own."

I blink and squint through the blur of my terror, and now I can see it's not a huge hound of hell that's cornered me, but two men that look like the Lindsay brothers come up from the village to hunt. My heart's still hammering, though, as they'll tell my Papa I was out in the dark, and then my secrets will come oozing out like the blood that's staining my thighs.

"Where are you from, little mistress?" the other man says. "Tell us your name and we'll take you home."

My heart leaps so hard in hope that I nearly cry out in pain. They haven't recognised me in the dark, and all I have to do is escape and I'll be home free, free, free with all my secret shame bundled away where no one can see it. The men's eyes are hungry, though, hungry like Agnes Naismith's eyes were yesterday morning when she came begging to buy bread with her oversweet words dripping from rotting plum lips. These men don't have sagging flesh like the old beggar woman, their skin is bleached in the pale moonlight and pulled so tight and gaunt they look like skeletons dug from the churchyard. Melted flesh or walking corpse, it makes no difference as everyone's hungry for secrets to trade for my family's favour, and I have to run if I want to keep mine hidden.

"What's that you've got there, little mistress? Are you out for the rabbits too?"

John Lindsay is leaning over me, reaching for my arm. The red cord is wrapped around my wrist again, trying to remind me that I've been bad, bad, bad and will never pass the gates of heaven. I shuffle away from the grasping hands, and feel the blood seeping into the back of my nightshirt as the soaking red rags are squeezed between my legs.

"Don't worry, little mistress, we mean you no harm," the other Lindsay brother says, but when I look up, I can see clearly now what he's carrying. There's a row of three strangled babes dangling on red cords, and he's holding the ends tight and grinning at me as they jerk and twitch at the end of the rope. I try to scream, but all that comes out is a raven's croak as my mouth is dry with fear and the blood in my veins has all drained out down my legs through my red, red rags. The birds high above do the screaming for me, their wails troubling the night air and fading to echoes that might just be faint memories locked away somewhere at the back of my mind. I know that James Lindsay's really holding rabbits from his trap, but all I can see are dead babes strangled in the dark, and I jump to my feet and run, run, run before my sins are discovered and I'm made to pay by being strung from a tree by my red curtain cord.

The world goes dark again and the terrible sounds in the sky fade until it's all just fog and fragments in my mind like a broken mirror that's been misted over by my panting breath.

Then it's daylight again, so sudden the shock of it feels like I've been plunged into a bowl of boiling water. The dawn sun is just peeking over the horizon, and I'm not in the forest but in my courtyard, my feet brown with mud, my thighs slick with blood, and purple marks up my numb arm where the red, red cord bit into my flesh in the night. It's gone from my wrist, and I don't know where, but there's no time to look now that it's daybreak. I turn to the kitchen door, ready to run back inside before the servants are up, but something stops me, a sight that sends me staggering back so fast I slip and fall on the cobblestones.

There are three ravens sitting on the kitchen doorstep, and their beaks are open in silent cries. Their eyes bulge wide with fear and pain, and for a moment I remember it all. I remember the three babes, and the red cord pulled taut between my hands as I struggle to undo the wicked work of the raven woman and the terrible things men and women do in the dark.

My scream is silent too as I fall back in a fit, my body jerking as though every devil's handmaiden is poking her needle into my skin at once. I don't feel Meg's soft hands as she gathers me up or hear her reassuring words. All I feel is blind terror as my mind fights to bury my sins deep where even I'll never find them again. And as Meg carries me indoors and up the stairs to bed before the rest of the household wakes, the only sound I can hear past the blood pounding in my veins is the cry of the ravens as they caw, caw, caw in condemnation.

Weft:

Thursday 7th June 1722

The crying of ravens was what woke Christian from her deep sleep. For a long moment she stood motionless, blinking in the dark and trying to work out where she was. She hadn't suffered a bout of sleepwalking since the terrible night she first fell ill at the age of eleven, but the tingle of fear that shivered down her spine when she discovered she was not tucked up in her own bed was every bit as keen and familiar as it had been two and half decades before.

Where..? What..? Christian's mind reeled, struggling to make sense of the half-remembered nightmare in the gloom of the unfamiliar surroundings. The storm had subsided but the wind was still wild, sending black clouds scudding across the face of the moon. Light flashed momentarily through the half-closed curtains, giving Christian a brief glimpse of the room she stood in.

It wasn't her own.

A figure lay in the bed before her, his muscular frame

a dark outline against the crisp white sheets.

"You're a woman now, and it's time to learn the facts of life," Katherine Campbell's voice seemed to echo in her head from far, far away. *"You need to know why men and women's bodies are shaped the way they are and what your monthly bleed is for."*

Christian covered her ears, but she couldn't shut out the sinister whispering that spoke of blood and bundles and the terrible things that men and women did in the dark. The worst thing was, there was a part of her that didn't want to, a part of her that even as a child had wanted to eat from the tree of knowledge and learn the women's secrets that had shone so temptingly in Katherine Campbell's eyes.

Against her will, her feet shuffled forward, carrying her closer to the figure in the bed. In another sudden flash of moonlight that lit up the guest room, Christian could see the rise and fall of Alexander Murray's chest as he slept. His nightshirt lay in a crumpled heap on the floor, and a small gasp escaped her lips at the sight of the dark hair curling up from bronzed skin pulled taut against his broad chest. The feeling of unease that had crept down Christian's spine settled in the pit of her stomach, mixing with a strangely alluring thrill, as though she were standing on the edge of a high cliff and every nerve was straining with the urge to jump.

Leaning over the bed now, her fingers gently brushed

the shadow of stubble forming on Alexander Murray's cheek, feeling their way gently across his jaw to stroke the lips that were turned enticingly up towards hers as he slept. Her own husband had aroused no passion in her during their short marriage, and that was why she had agreed to wed the stolid minister. He had been safe, pious, celibate, no searching hands to disturb her sleep in the night, nor incontinent thoughts to trouble her dreams. But this man, once stripped of his foppish ornaments and powdered wig, was indeed a creature to stir the senses and awaken passions that had lain dormant in Christian's hidden subconscious.

The terrible things that men and women do in the dark...

As Christian leaned in, her lips tantalisingly close to the warm skin beneath her, her hand moved down to caress the neck laid bare against the pillow. And that was when she saw it. A red curtain cord, wrapped tight around her wrist, ready for the deed that must be done to preserve her purity.

It wasn't the scream that Christian managed to stifle just in time that shook the night air, but the cry of a raven perched on the windowsill, watching her every move through the glass.

The throb of desire in the pit of her stomach burst like a blister over burned flesh, and she felt a hot rush as it drained away, leaving her empty and shivering in the dark.

No, no, no! the child's voice cried in her mind, joining the raven's lament on her lost innocence. Numb with dread. Christian looked down. In the next flash of moonlight from behind the clouds, she could see the red stain blossoming on her nightdress between her thighs, her guilt laid bare for all the world to see. As the room was plunged into shadow once more, a fog seemed to fill Christian's mind, cutting her conscious thought off from the actions that came next.

She was unaware of stepping forward again, each motion now smooth and self-assured. Her hand moved, unbidden, to her wrist, unwrapping the waiting cord and flexing it between purposeful fingers. This time as she reached for the sleeping man's neck, there would be no tenderness, this fresh desire sprung from a deeper, more murky pool. The red cord tightened between her hands, ready for the work they half remembered from nightmares of the past.

It was another hand that stilled them before they could carry out the terrible deed. Christian shuddered as tender but firm fingers closed around her wrist where the curtain cord had once been.

"Come away, Mistress Shaw," a voice whispered urgently in her ear. "You mustn't be seen here."

Meg! My faithful Meg has come to save me from my sins!

Her maid's reassuring presence was a candle in the dark, shining through the fog in Christian's mind and lighting her way back to her own room. She was barely aware of the capable hands as they steadied her faltering steps, changed her stained nightdress and stuffed the rags she hadn't needed in twenty-five years between her legs before laying her down on the bed. Through the dark red mist in her mind, Christian could feel rather than see the calming figure pulling out the small trundle bed beneath her own and settling down to sleep within easy reach if her mistress needed her again in the night.

The wailing wind had died down to a whisper, and the raven had ceased its terrible cry, but it was the howl of despair from her own mind that filled the silence they left behind.

No, no, no! the child whimpered in the fog. *It's happening again!*

But Christian was no longer a little girl. She was a full-grown woman with a keen mind and a will of iron. *I can beat this!* her own voice shouted back. *I conquered you before, and I'll not rest until I've beaten you again.* This time there would be no descent into madness, no sacrifices made to regain her sanity. This time would be different.

By morning she was mistress of her thoughts once more, and she knew what she had to do.

By the time the first rays of dawn were glinting on the horizon and Meg was stirring from her sleep on the trundle bed, Christian had already packed her bag and was waiting impatiently for the day ahead.

"Come, Meg," she said, the steady tone of command back in her voice despite the pallor of her cheeks. "Ready yourself. We need to leave early."

Awake at once, Meg glanced at the stained nightdress bundled under the bed next to the chamber pot full of bloody rags. Allowing no words of surprise to pass her lips, no look of anxiety that might disturb her mistress to crease her brow, she merely asked, "Where are we going, Mistress Shaw?"

"To the clootie well of St Fillan's," Christian replied. She need say no more. Meg knew the significance of the holy site.

"I'll let Thomas know we need the horse and trap." Meg dressed quickly, slipping out to rouse the servant who slept above the stables. By the time Christian had been to the kitchen to fetch bread, cheese, and a jug of leftover milk, the horse and cart were standing in the laneway, and the other servants were stirring, ready for their morning chores.

"Mary, tell my mother I'm going to Paisley to seek a buyer for my thread," she told the kitchen maid who blinked in surprise at seeing her mistress leave so early. Christian was often up at the crack of dawn to work on her spinning or check on her bleaching, but the journey to Paisley was not so long that she'd needed to leave without breakfasting first. Mary knew better than to question her mistress, though, and she merely gave a short curtsy and went about her morning chores without comment.

Thomas raised an eyebrow when Christian told him their destination, but he too knew the value of silence as far as this particular mistress was concerned. She would pay him well for this trip, and what did it matter to him whether he said they'd been to Paisley instead of St Fillan's? Christian was well aware that her infamous past earned her more obedience from the servants than loyalty, respect or love.

A single flick of the reins set them in motion, and as Christian watched Bargarran House fade into the distance, she felt the sudden enormity of what had happened hit her.

I haven't bled in twenty-five years! she thought in shock. *Why now, after all this time?* Half-remembered images crowded her mind, threatening to overwhelm her, and she pushed them back with an effort, burying them again with sheer force of will. She would not remember the past. She would not remember last night. And she would not, no matter how much the ravens taunted her, remember the significance of the red cord around her wrist. All that mattered now was reaching the holy well, and praying for the forgiveness of her sins and the deliverance from evil she so badly needed.

The fields, farmsteads and labourers whirled past in a blur of motion as Thomas kept the horse going at a good clip despite the bumpy road, and even though the sun was much higher in the sky by the time he turned off the main road, Christian had been so lost in her own thoughts she felt as though no time had passed at all.

"You'd best go on foot from here, Widow Millar," Thomas said, halting the horse under the shade of a tree. "Meg will show you the way." It was his way of letting her know that he was willing to keep up the pretence that she'd never been here before, and Christian was grateful for it, clumsy as it was. There were many local preachers who still frowned on the ancient well as a place of pagan superstition, and one had gone so far as to have it filled in with stones during Christian's early childhood. Little by little, stone by secret stone, the villagers had dug it out again, and now they kept their visits to the ancient spring quiet in case they incurred a more permanent sanction from the church.

"This way, Mistress Shaw," Meg said, helping Christian down from the cart and making her way carefully through the dense press of trees. Christian knew the way as well as her maid did, but the rags between her legs slowed her down, forcing her to take small mincing steps for fear of allowing any tell-tale leaks to stain her dress.

The trees gave way to a glade around a hollow, a bubbling spring flowing from beneath a large rock to fill the deep pool. If it was just the water the local people came to drink and bathe in, the church might not have been so critical of the ancient rituals, but it was the other practice that aroused the greater part of their ire. On the branches of the great oak overhanging the pool, a thousand pieces of rag were tied, their ends flapping gently in the breeze. Each was a silent prayer for intercession – a wish for health, wealth, happiness or children – made by the sick, the poor, the lonely or the hopeful. Christian was none of those things, but she felt she needed the healing powers of the waters more than any who had come before her.

"Do you have what you need, Mistress Shaw?" Meg asked. When Christian nodded in reply, Meg withdrew, retreating into the trees to give her mistress privacy. She had not needed it before. On previous visits to the well, Christian had merely come to drink the healing waters as a tonic, to raise her depressed spirits, to calm her troubled dreams, or to pray. But this time was different. This time the rag that she tied to the tree was not shining white, but grubby pink, despite her best efforts to scrub it clean with soft soap.

Let it stop! she prayed with all her might as she wrapped the end of the linen around the nearest branch. *Please, let it stop!*

Her dreams were bleeding into reality, and if she couldn't stem the flow, then the past might catch up with her, becoming the present. She shuddered as she eased her undergarments down, letting the bundle of stained rags sink to the bottom of the well and lifting her skirts high to step into the pool. The cooling water crept up her thighs as she ventured deeper, until it was almost to her waist.

Gazing down into the clear pool, she could just make out the dirty bundle of rags at the bottom before the slow ooze of red between her thighs befouled the water.

Taint, Christian thought in disgust. *Rot. Corruption.* Those were the words the clergy had whispered behind their hands during her long illness, when Christian had pulled straw, chicken feather, and even dung from her mouth to prove to the world she was bewitched. The young doctor had used other, longer words she didn't understand, but anything was better than having them guess the real cause of her affliction, and finding out what she had done.

But what did I do? Christian wondered, a sudden memory of a red cord flashing through her mind. *And where did I wander to last night?*

Before she could flinch from the hidden thoughts that flickered like fire at the edges of her consciousness, a sudden cry shook the air. Christian looked up.

A black raven was sitting on the branch of the oak tree, her wet rag held in its beak. The linen was no longer mottled white and pink but scarlet red, soaked with fresh blood that drip, drip, dripped into the pool, carrying Christian's thoughts down the deep well of her mind to the very bottom.

Warp:

Saturday 14th November 1696

There's an early fall of snow outside, soft as a whisper, over in a moment, but I can watch the brief flash of flakes through the window from my bed and my heart hurts with longing when I see how pure white they are. My sheets in this strange bed in Glasgow are white too – not so white as the snow, but white enough to make my heart sing with health if it wasn't for the treatment the doctors have been using to cure my affliction.

Every time I think I'm recovering, and my mind is starting to piece together the fragments it was broken into by Katherine Campbell's words, Agnes Naismith's hungry eyes and the raven woman's red, red rag, it happens again. The doctor comes with his small metal jaws that tear at my flesh, and the bowl is stained with blood mixed with guilt and sin. It's not the stale beef man's teeth that are biting me now that we've come to Glasgow for help. The doctor here is handsome and famous and smells of crushed mint, but his teeth are every bit as sharp, and their bite has the very same effect.

I see red and I remember for a moment what I've done, and before I can stop myself my body is twitching and jerking, tormented with such pain it feels like the devil himself is stabbing me with his pitchfork over and over until I'm halfway to hell. In those awful moments I see the faces of all those who might have guessed my secrets dancing before my eyes, and I can't help but scream their names until my throat is raw as uncooked meat and gasping for breath so hard I'm near dead by the time it's over.

Margaret Lang comes first. It was the raven woman who started it all with her red rag on the bed and her feather fingers that lifted the meaty bundle by candlelight. Katherine Campbell comes next, with her wicked words and the glint in her eyes that filled my soul with such terror as she ran through the grass to tell my secret shame to Mama. Then comes Agnes Naismith with her hungry eyes that spied out my lost innocence by morning light, and the Lindsay brothers who sniffed out my crimes by moonlight. There are others too who came later, their names all jumbled in my head and the reasons I fear them as confused as my tumbling thoughts. I only know that they mustn't be allowed to tell the world what I've done, even though I don't know myself what I've done until those awful moments when the crushed mint man bites me with his metal jaws and the red mist descends once more.

The door opens and he comes back in, this time with more visitors who've come to see me perform my tricks with bones and coal and other bits of trash. I mustn't disappoint them or the crushed mint man might start to guess the real reason for my screaming fits and jerking limbs, and then it won't be witchcraft, but my own wickedness that's blamed for my afflictions.

I'm lucky that Mama and Papa aren't with them today, for if they watch my tricks one too many times they might see they're all a show. But a show is what these rich friends of the crushed mint man all want, and I'm ready to perform. So while Mama's in her bed, exhausted by another night of sitting up with me, and Papa's in town consulting with the senior clergy, I'll be here coughing up bits and bones and nails and nastiness to make my name as the girl who was bewitched, and all the while my secrets will be safely hidden from all the eyes that watch my antics but can't guess where they come from.

Meg closes the door behind her, coming to sit quietly by the side of my bed, as she always does. Nobody notices Meg. She's not pretty or rich or important, she's just a servant who cleans up my vomit and silently washes my wet sheets long after the doctors and clergy and important people have all left. No one will see if she slips me anything under the bed sheets while they all have their eyes fixed on me.

She doesn't need to hand me anything today, though, it's all been prepared in advance. She sewed a small pocket in my nightdress to hide small items, and there's another in my pillowcase for anything else I might need for my performance. The crushed mint man checks my pulse and my heart and my breathing, but he doesn't check my linen. That's women's work, and he's too important for that.

The rich people all settle down for the performance but I don't begin right away, or that would make them suspicious. Instead I answer their questions: where am I from, who are my parents, what do I think is happening to me? I don't fear their questions the way I feared the oversweet words of Agnes Naismith. They can't spy out my secrets the way the red-rimmed eyes of the beggar woman did the morning my mind began to unravel in earnest. I recite my Catechism for them to prove I'm a good, pious girl, and I spout all the Bible verses I know to show how seriously I've been taking my Sunday studies. Meg says that will help my case when the time comes, but I don't know what she means as I don't know what my case is or what's going to come in time. All I know, is that until I'm well again and mistress of my own body and thoughts, I have to keep up the pretence to make sure no one guesses my terrible secrets.

The crushed mint man's important guests are growing

restless. One fat man is yawning, and a fine lady is fanning her face. The doctor keeps the fire in here hot as he says I should sweat out my fever, but it makes my head ache and I long for the chance to be out in the flutter of new-fallen snow catching the cooling flakes on my tongue like I'm a little girl again and not this half-way thing between child and woman who's continually caught in the crushed mint man's teeth.

It's time to begin the show.

First, I arch my back, rolling my eyes to prove I'm in pain. I try to remember what it's like for real when I'm bitten by the crushed mint man's metal jaws, but he's sitting on the far side of the room taking notes in a little book, and my memories of those times are all confused, so I just have to pretend. Next I start coughing like there's something coming up from my lungs, then I spit out the pieces of straw, feathers and small bones I hid in my cheeks before the crushed mint man came in with his guests. They're all wide awake and interested now, waiting to see what I'm going to produce next.

This is the bit where I have to be careful, or I'll get caught acting. I put my hands in my mouth and choke like there's something big stuck there, but really I'm cramming my fingers down my throat the way Meg showed me so I can throw up the soup I was given for lunch. I retch a few times, then it all comes rushing up in a mess of potato and leek and barley broth. I spew it into my hands, and time it just right so no one can see the piece of coal I sneaked from my pillowcase with one hand while they were all watching the other hand pull things from my mouth.

The coal is still hot from the fire where I got it just before the crushed mint man and his guests came in. It'll have burned a hole through my bed linen, but that's alright as Meg will fix it with her sewing needle and clever fingers before anyone can notice.

The crushed mint man throws down his book and snatches the coal from my slimy hands, holding it up in triumph like it's a rare gem from one of those faraway lands I've read about in the Bible. "It's still hot!" he cries, as though it's a wonderful thing that a girl my age is throwing up burning coals instead of being something to be afeared of. The fine lady with the fan actually starts to clap, until the fat man beside her scowls her into silence. The fat man must be a doctor too, as he's taking notes in his little book, and his yawns are all gone, replaced by wide eyes and scribbles and endless questions he asks of everyone except me.

Now that the show's over, it's as though I'm not here anymore, and it's the lump of still-warm coal that takes centre stage, passed around like it's something precious. The fine people don't want to look at me now that I'm covered in sick and there's bones and feathers and straw sticking to my sheets.

When they're done discussing me, the crushed mint man takes his fine guests out, and I shudder when he closes the door after them, as I know he'll be back later with his metal jaws and his big white bowl to bite my arm and drain my blood and send me spinning off into madness for real. My stomach's churning, and I don't know whether it's from the fingers down my throat or the fear of the metal jaws, but before I can work myself up into a panic, Meg's there for me, wiping my brow before the sweat can run down and sting my eyes.

"Did I do that right?" I ask her as she cleans up the mess of bones and straw and vomit from the bed. She holds my hand and strokes my hair and smiles at me more sweetly than Mama's ever smiled at me in her whole life.

"That was perfect, Mistress Shaw. It won't be long now before those who did this to you are brought to justice."

I'm tired and aching, and all in a muddle as I don't know for sure anymore what came first – the sickness or the fear of discovery, or whether the people I've accused cursed me or whether I cursed them, but it doesn't matter now. All that matters is that it's soon going to be over, and I'll be well again, and if I stay good and pure and innocent, then I won't need the rags, or the raven woman, and I'll never push a meaty bundle down the tunnel of sin in the dark or need the red, red cord to undo the raven woman's wicked work on me.

Weft:

Friday 8th June 1722

Christian usually enjoyed walking around the Bargarran estate at sunrise, before the servants and labourers rose to work and spoiled the silence with their rowdy shouts and raucous laughter. But not this morning. Yesterday's trip to the clootie well had not produced the desired result, and Christian could feel the blood slowly seeping into her rags as she crossed the courtyard, heading for the far fields. The dull ache in her head had spread to her stomach, knots of cramp twisting her guts with every step that she took.

Witch. Witch. Witch. Witch...

Her shoes beat out the slow tattoo on the cobblestones, a dire warning that time had come full circle and the past was repeating itself. But who was the witch who was causing her suffering now, twenty-five years after she'd had all those who tormented her mind and troubled her dreams put to death? Who could possibly wish her harm after everything she'd done to atone for her past sins and bring honour to her family's name through her hard work?

Christian leaned heavily on the courtyard gate, clutching her side and taking a long, shaky breath. The overgrown rowan branches caught at her dress, and even now, in her weakened state, she made a mental note to ask Thomas to trim the archway. Nothing must be neglected, not a single task must be overlooked, however small, that might make others suspect she was no longer mistress of herself or capable or running the estate. Otherwise there might be talk of her marrying again, to bring a man's steadying hand to Bargarran House.

Christian shuddered, a brief memory of fingers caressing dark hair and stroking sleeping lips flashing through her head, before it was gone, leaving her blinking and confused in the faint morning light.

No, she didn't need a man's help despite her temporary weakness. She would do this alone, and keep the estate running in good order, just the way her father had done, and his father before him. She glanced back at the byres, checking that the horseshoes her father had nailed there during her childhood illness were still in place. They were rusting now, the metal tarnished and chipped, and she added replacing them to the list of chores for Thomas when she returned to the house. The charms hadn't stopped witches from weaving their wicked web around her family all those years ago. Katherine Campbell had come and gone from the byres as she pleased, right up until she'd been falsely accused of stealing milk. Agnes Naismith had stepped into the courtyard despite the rowan branches trained around the gate, and Margaret Lang had marched past the rowan around the doors and tied her red rag on her mother's bed, bold as brass. Still, even if they couldn't protect her house from those determined to do her family harm, Christian felt better knowing the tokens were kept in good order, just in case.

She took a deep breath and pushed the gate open, striding more confidently now across the fields to survey the estate. She couldn't afford to take small mincing steps or clutch her stomach out here in the open; any farm workers who observed her must see that nothing was wrong, and that she was mistress of herself as well as of them.

The field nearest the house was used for her thread whitening experiments, and the grass there was scrubby and yellowed, testament to lye overflowing from the barrels during the first and second bleachings. Christian was itching to check on the progress of the thread soaking in the buttermilk in the bleaching barn, but there were still several more days to go until she could remove it, and she didn't want to disturb the process until it was completed.

The nearest fields were planted with barley, the stalks

still short but growing strongly. A good summer of sun, and there would be a fine harvest this year. But it was the flax fields that Christian was most interested in. This year's crop would need to be a bumper one. She needed a steady supply for her spinning wheels, and with finances being so tight, she couldn't afford to buy a new batch from other sources until her thread started selling.

It won't sell until it's white enough, Christian thought, clutching her crucifix in frustration. She could only pray she'd perfected the bleaching process this time, but somehow, deep down, she knew her latest effort would fall short of her ideal, just like all the rest.

Maybe if I tried—

"Good morning, Widow Millar," a wheezing voice interrupted her thoughts. Christian looked round to see an old woman standing by the low row of hedges that stopped the cattle from trampling the flax. She popped early summer berries into her mouth one by one as she filled her basket, and Christian watched, transfixed as the red juice ran down her chin and stained her faded plaid.

The old woman's face is lined and yellow like folded parchment, and the ragged clothes are hanging from her bones like tears weeping down her frail body. She's shoving berries into her mouth as fast as her shaking hands can manage, and the juice drips red, red, red from her hungry cavern as she mashes them desperately in empty gums. I stand stock still in shock, my bloody nightdress clutched in my hands for all the world to see and with the dry one I've thrown on stained pink from yesterday's washing. I can't get to the river to wash my nightdress and rags as the old woman's standing in the way, and now she's seen my secret shame and is pointing, pointing, pointing, with her hands all running red and her mouth a bloody smear of accusation and her eyes lit up in triumph now she has the power over me to—

"Is something wrong, Widow Millar?" the old woman said, seeing the strange look that passed across Christian's face. "I'm sorry if you think me taking the berries is a liberty, I should have asked at the house first, but I thought—"

"Maggie?" Christian blinked, the rising sun dazzling her eyes for a moment as it cleared the horizon.

The old woman looked confused. "No, Widow Millar, I'm Anne Herries – Tam Herries' wife?" She made it sound like a question, but Christian already knew the answer. She'd been mistaken. The old woman wasn't Maggie Fulton. That old beggar woman had died long, long ago in the witch fires on the Gallow Green.

Without replying, Christian turned and walked away, her steps less certain and assured now. She'd been convinced as a child that Maggie Fulton had been pointing out her shame that morning down by the river, in the terrible week before she fell ill. Now, looking back with an adult's eyes, Christian saw more.

The old woman's fingers weren't pointing, they were cupped, beseeching. The shrivelled lips weren't open in a cry of triumph, they were gasping the word 'please'. And the light in the rheumy eyes that morning had not been the glitter of discovery that might lead to power, but the gleam of hope that might lead to help.

She hadn't been pointing out Christian's shame. She's been asking for alms.

Christian crouched in the long grass, feeling suddenly faint. How many others had she condemned unfairly during that brief period of madness, when up was down, and black and white were red, red, red?

They were all witches! a child's voice piped up from the back of her mind. *They caused my suffering. They had to die so I could get better.*

But did they? What came first, and what came last? And that long, long period in the middle when Christian was in bed being bled by doctors and pressed to perform her tricks for the clergy to prove the witchcraft they were so desperate to discover, who was to blame for that?

Christian laid her head on her knee, breathing hard and trying to still her troubled mind. The waves of her past were crashing on the shores of her present, and she was slowly drowning in the rising tide. How long she sat there with her eyes closed she couldn't say, but when she finally raised her head, the sun was much higher in the sky, and the sound of tuneless whistling was coming from the fields where the labourers had got to work.

Christian stood up, careful not to let them see her, but not carefully enough. She'd forgotten for a moment that the curse was back upon her, and she had a bundle of wet rags to nurse. She groaned in despair as the distant memory of blood trickling down her leg became her new reality, staining the pale yellow of her dress with a crimson blush. She should have chosen her clothes more judiciously this morning, she should have remembered to bring a plaid to hide any tell-tale stains.

She crept back to the house through the long grass, her head bent in shame and her thighs pressed tight together to avoid any further leaks. The damage was done, however, and now she'd have to find a way past the servants in the kitchen and hall without being spotted.

The thunder of hooves on the laneway made her glance up despite her self-consciousness, and she saw a rider on a fine grey horse galloping towards the house as though his life depended on it.

Alexander Murray.

It seemed the awkward dinner the other night had not been enough to deter him, and her sister's smiles had cast the desired spell, despite Elizabeth's sour looks and Isabella's cruelty. Alexander Murray was clearly a man on a mission, and at this time of the morning, that could only mean a proposal of marriage.

Christian bent over in the screen of grass and retched.

What in God's name is wrong with me? she shivered. *I should be happy for my sister!*

The long red cloak Alexander Murray wore streamed behind him, a scarlet train that seemed to Christian to burn with desire and longing in the golden glow of morning. Memories crowded unbidden into her head, pushing their way through locked doors long weakened by worry and lack of sleep. It wasn't this horse she saw in her mind's eye, but one like it, not this man that first stirred the cauldron of passion bubbling inside her, but another. She closed her eyes, and remembered.

I'm sitting on the kitchen steps in the courtyard even though I should be in my room hiding from the world until the danger is passed and my rags are no longer red. But I can't see him clearly through the window, and I want him to smile at me up close nearly as much as I want my girlish innocence back before Katherine Campbell whispered her wicked words in my head and laid this curse upon me.

Papa's summoned the blacksmith to shoe the horses, and his eyes are dark as raven's wings and his smock is rolled so far up his arms I can see the curve of every muscle in his strong shoulders as he lifts the horse's leg and examines her hoof. He looks up and sees me watching him, and my stomach flutters strangely when he flashes me a smile with teeth whiter than Mama's best china tea set.

He looks down again, setting the iron shoe in place over the horse's hoof and positioning the first nail, but when he reaches for his hammer he sees he's left it leaning up by the stable door. Instead of putting the horse's hoof down and going to get it, he flashes me another smile. "Would you do me the honour of lending a hand, little mistress? he asks.

For even a hint of that smile that makes my insides quiver, I'd fight my way through a pack of hungry dogs quarrelling over a single bone, but all I have to do to earn it is skip across the courtyard and pick up a hammer. I'm halfway across the cobblestones before I remember I'm not a girl anymore, and my red rags are leaking onto my gown at the sudden careless movement.

My hand is shaking as it closes over the hammer, and I'm scared to turn around as there's a small spot on the front of my dress that might bloom into a flower if I move too fast.

"Mistress Shaw?" John Reid reaches for the hammer with his free hand that's not holding onto the horse's hoof, and when his fingers brush mine I get such a shock of excitement and fear I snatch my arm back with a cry.

The horse is startled, rearing up and knocking the blacksmith clear off his feet. I run back to the kitchen, feeling the red rags come loose and the blood seeping into my dress. I make the mistake of turning at the door to check the horse hasn't trampled John Reid all to pieces. He sitting up on the cobblestones, pulling the nail out of his palm while the horse charges off to the far fields, and there's blood dripping down his fingers that's red as the stain on my dress. His eyes meet mine and he's no longer smiling, there's a frown on his face and he knows he knows he knows that I'm no longer a little girl now, and he's got the power to break me just like he broke the horse that's bolting for freedom. I run for freedom too, but there's nowhere to hide, the eyes are everywhere and the world is red instead of white and the ravens are crying, crying, crying, and—

Christian gritted her teeth and pushed the memory away, running now for the shelter of the house before the rider could block her way back through the courtyard. She could feel the stain on her dress growing, but she dare not stop nor look down. She had to get back to her room, back to Meg, who would make everything spotless and safe again.

The gate was still open, and she raced through, skidding to a halt on the cobblestones. The courtyard wasn't empty. But it wasn't a servant who looked up from the pile of roses she was stripping petals off to make rose water. It was Elizabeth.

Her sister's mouth formed a small 'o' of surprise at Christian's dishevelled appearance, which quickly changed to a grimace of disgust and pity as she saw the red stain blossoming on her sister's dress. Christian could feel the blood pounding in her veins, her heart echoing the beat of the approaching horse's hooves.

She knows she knows she knows! the child's voice cried in her head. *Elizabeth knows and the rider will know and the ravens are watching my every move and wailing my secrets to the world, and soon everyone will know that I'm impure and wicked and I'm the one stealing through the night with the red cord around my wrist to undo the raven woman's work in the dark and—*

Just as Alexander Murray came cantering into the courtyard, Christian reached out and pushed Elizabeth into the path of his horse.

There was a cry of fear, a shout of surprise, and a startled neigh as the horse reared up, throwing its rider off and bringing its hooves down on the head of the woman in its path. Christian watched, numb and detached, as two figures rolled to the ground and lay still, their blood running down the cracks between the cobblestones while the terrified horse raced through the open gate and across the fields.

Then, slowly and deliberately, she picked up her sister's fallen plaid, wrapping it around her waist to hide the stain on her dress before slipping silently back through the house as her mother and Jean and the servants came swarming into the courtyard to scream and scream and scream.

Warp:

Saturday 9th January 1697

The snow outside is white and the baby's linen is white, but the raven on the windowsill has eyes that are black as they watch me unwrap the red, red cord from my wrist and lean over the crib. The doctor's metal jaws have finished their work for the day and my arm is swollen, but it's strong enough to do what has to be done to undo the raven woman's work here in my own house.

Through the strange fog that descended as my blood drained into the doctor's bowl, I could hear the baby crying, crying, crying, and it set my teeth on edge and sent spasms of pain through my body. For a few brief moments it all became clear – I'd undone the raven woman's work in the nearby houses, but here in my own, the evidence of the red, red rag on the bed was howling its little head off and telling the world that I'd never know peace until I'd reset the clock to a time before Mama's meaty bundle and the whispered words in the dark stole my innocence.

I flex the curtain cord between my fingers, wrapping it around Jean's neck, once, twice for good measure. Mama will cry and the nursemaid will cry and little Lizzie will cry and cry and cry, but then there'll be calm and this constant wailing hole in my head where my reason once was will be filled with silence and I'll finally know peace.

My hands clench, gripping the cord tight, and I—

A hand closes around my arm, strong but gentle, stilling me before the cord tightens.

"Come away, Mistress Shaw," a voice whispers urgently in my ear. "You mustn't be seen here."

Meg! My faithful Meg has come to save me from my sins!

The red mist thickens to white fog, and the last thing I see clearly is Meg unwrapping the curtain cord from the sleeping baby's neck and putting it in her own pocket. I instantly forget what it's for and why I'm here, and now all I know is that I'm cold and shivering and the ice clinging to the window where the raven once sat has clawed its way inside my heart and is chilling me to the bone.

Everything seems very distant and dreamlike, and the only thing that's near and real is Meg with her arms around me, but maybe she's not a maid guiding me to my room, maybe she's an angel flying me to heaven on her soft white wings. But then I get confused as we're down instead of up and I forget which way the stairs go and how my legs work and it's only when Papa comes striding down the hall and lifts me in his strong arms that I know for sure I'm going back to my room where the doctor and his metal jaws will bite me before I can get well again.

"Is she still sleepwalking?" I hear Papa ask from the faraway place beyond the fog.

"Yes," Meg replies, floating somewhere by my side just out of reach. "I think it might be best to have the babe moved to your cousin's house until my poor mistress is cured, sir. Little Jean's cries have been disturbing her in the night, and I don't think the doctor's draughts are working."

Papa makes a strange noise in his throat, but I can't see his face so I don't know if he's angry or sad or just suffering from indigestion after dinner. "Men of science can't cure what ails her," he says. "It's the church we must look to, to save Christian's soul as much as her earthly body."

Even in my muddled state, I know my Meg well enough to see clear through the mist that's she's hesitating before asking her next question, afraid of overstepping her place. For my sake, though, she overcomes her fears and asks, "Do you mean, sir, that they'll investigate the witches who did this to my poor mistress?"

"Yes," Papa says, too tired to play the ninth Laird now and too grateful for all Meg's done for me to chastise her for prying. "The Paisley Presbytery met at the end of December, and they've agreed to set up a Commission to investigate Christian's case. They're gathering evidence now – Doctor Brisbane will come down from Glasgow to present his findings. As for the accused, well, they'll damn themselves with their own wicked words."

From through the black night and red mist and from far, far away, I can see that Meg is smiling as Papa lays me down on my white, white linen to sleep.

Weft:

Sunday 10th June 1722

"Do you think she'll recover, Doctor?" Christian's words were cold, business-like, no trace of emotion betraying her inner feelings.

The doctor checked Elizabeth's pulse once more, then laid her pale hand on the bed. "There's certainly more cause for hope than there was yesterday morning," he said, weighing his words carefully as he put away his instruments. "The surgeon has done a skilful job in setting her skull, and if the bones heal, then there's every reason for optimism."

Christian looked down at the still figure on the bed. Elizabeth had never been pretty, but with her hair shaved off and a mass of bandages covering the jagged scars across her head where her bones had fractured, her pinched face had taken on the waxen look of a death mask hanging in a mausoleum. "I'm not asking for platitudes, I'm asking for your medical opinion," Christian said frostily. She had never got over her loathing of doctors, and this one's oily manner was getting under her skin and making her itch to be rid of him.

One glance was all the doctor needed to be sure that Christian was made of sterner stuff than her mother and youngest sister. "Well," he sighed, "if I'm being honest, even if she recovers, there's bound to be impairment with an injury this severe."

"What kind of impairment?" Christian pressed on, relentlessly. "Will she remember what happened to her?"

The doctor threw her a pitying look and heaved another sigh. "It's possible she'll regain her movement and some degree of speech in time," he said, "but she won't be the woman she was before."

"I see. Thank you, Doctor."

Her face was expressionless as she opened the door and called Elizabeth's maid back in. Despite how badly the girl had been treated by her sister, the maid was loyal and caring, and Christian hadn't wanted the truth of Elizabeth's condition spread all over the house. Better they all remain ignorant, clinging to hope, rather than wasting precious work hours fretting over something that couldn't be fixed.

"And Alexander Murray's family?" the doctor asked as they stepped out into the hallway. "Have they been informed?"

"His sister is unfortunately staying with her in-laws

up in Inverness at present," Christian said, her voice flat and empty as though all of the life had been drained from it. "A rider was dispatched at the first opportunity yesterday morning, but I doubt he'll be able to catch them on the road, so the earliest we can expect their return is tomorrow. We will look after the body until then."

The body the body the body…

The body is strangely beautiful despite being bent and broken, and I can't help but run my hands across the curling hairs on its chest as I wash the last of the blood away. I've sent Mary to the kitchen for a fresh bowl of water, and Janet and Bess are busy cleaning and mending Master Murray's fine shirt so we can dress him again, and I'm alone with the body the body the body and there's something burning my insides as I touch the cold flesh in the back sitting room where no one can see me. I don't know how it came to be here – one minute it was on a horse, the next the beast was rearing up and knocking poor Elizabeth over because my silly sister must've chosen to stand in its way just to spite Master Murray for loving Jeanie instead of her. However it happened, the body's here now, and I have it all to myself to explore with my washcloth and fingers that go dancing, dancing, dancing across the once-warm skin all the way down to—

Christian clenched her fists, forcing her nails deep

into her flesh to regain control of the thoughts that were threatening to spiral beyond her reach. "Thank you, Doctor, I know you've had a long night. If you go with Meg, she'll take you to the kitchen for some refreshments."

The doctor nodded gratefully, following the maid downstairs and leaving Christian to choose what information to pass on to her mother and youngest sister. Christian didn't stay with them long. Jean was still in the first throes of passionate grief for the man she nursed a warm affection for despite his foppery, and her mother was overcome with the thought of losing her surest way to financial stability and comfort in her old age.

"The doctor thinks that Elizabeth will recover," Christian told them, trying to make herself heard above the sounds of sobbing that filled Jean's room. "So that's something to be thankful for."

"But how could this have happened?" her mother wailed. "Master Murray was always such a fine rider, so good with horses – how could his mare have thrown him like that?"

Her face was screwed up in anguish, and Christian struggled to find words that would comfort her. "I told you, Mother," she said more harshly than she meant to, "Elizabeth slipped on the cobblestones and fell in front of the horse. It got a fright and bucked. It was just an accident."

Christian was sure that was what had happened, but there was a strange hole in her mind that seemed to have opened up just as Alexander Murray was riding into the courtyard. Elizabeth must have slipped. There was no other explanation for her falling in front of the horse like that. Every time she tried to conjure the memory of the event it slipped away, and all she could hear in her mind was the cawing of ravens on the rooftops and a distant scream that echoed up from the cavern in her mind.

The ravens were still cawing so loudly Christian thought she would go mad. They hadn't let up for two whole nights, and she hadn't got a wink of sleep between directing the servants, helping the surgeon, and washing the fresh corpse for the wake. Perhaps it was just her frayed nerves that made their throaty calls seem so piercing, but still, Christian had the eerie feeling they were trying to warn her of something.

"How are we going to manage now?" Her mother was still knee-deep in her own self-pity, lamenting the lost wealth and status the marriage would have brought. "How will we get by?"

"By hard work. Mostly mine!" Christian snapped, irritated beyond reason by her mother's inability to function in a crisis and the maddening noise of the birds on the rooftops. "We've already lost two days' labour, and the doctor's keeping the servants too busy for them to attend to the bleaching barrels."

"Oh, Christian! How can you think of your thread at a time like this?" It was Jean who aimed this rebuke at her, her eyes glistening with angry tears. "And on a Sunday too!"

"One of us has to," Christian threw over her shoulder as she marched out of the room, unable to bear the claustrophobic fog of crying and cawing any longer. She escaped to the one place she knew she'd find peace, the place she'd been longing to return to all through the long nights of waking watchfulness.

She didn't make it to the library before another vision overtook her.

She was just passing down the long hallway when the sun emerged from behind a fluffy white cloud, its full summer glory pouring through one of the high windows and pooling on the floor before her. A memory emerged from the shimmering patch of light – an echo of moonbeams hitting the same spot one early February at the height of Christian's illness.

Christian stumbled, clutching the wall for support as half-forgotten images tumbled through her mind.

"Please, Christian, go to bed. You'll wear yourself out with all this pacing."

Baby Jeanie's been sent away so her cries don't keep me up at night, but it's the phantom cries in my mind that are holding sleep at bay and sending me half wild with fear as I pace the hallways and stairs to escape the awful wailing.

There's nowhere to go – the babes with the red cord round their necks and their faces turned crimson are following me through the candlelit passageways, crying out that I've done something bad bad bad even though Meg tells me I'm good good good and I can't remember whether I'm a saint or a sinner or just a mad girl running through the house with her head on fire.

The sight of a figure standing at the door to the library makes me stop my dizzying steps.

The moon is bright and I can see it's one of Papa's tenant farmers. John Lindsay of Barloch should hold no fear for me, seeing as I've known him forever and his wife fed me apple pie after she found me lost in the woods when I crossed the fields on my own aged four. He doesn't know my secret, he's never seen my shame, yet something about him makes me clutch Mama's hand and gasp in horror.

"What's he doing here?" I hiss as father opens the library door and welcomes John with a handshake even though it's night time and it's late for visitors.

"He'll just be here to ask your father for money." Mama tries to soothe me. "Come away to bed, Christian."

Money..?

My head is reeling and I can't think straight. I don't recall that it's a lean time of year for farmers and they need help to tide them over until spring. I don't remember that John is here at the same time every year asking for a loan to keep his family fed until the lambing season. All I can focus on is the fact that John is wearing a red cord around his waist to hold up his breeches, and it's the very one I lost running through the fields that last night I can't remember. He's here for money, so that must mean he's found out the awful secret I can't remember and he's going to make Papa buy his silence with all the coin he owns.

"Little mistress, what's the matter?"

John is looking at me now, and I don't see concern in his eyes, I just see cunning and greed as he glances first at me and then at Papa, readying himself to sell his silence to the highest bidder. I have to act fast or he'll tell my terrible sins to Papa, but I don't know what to do and I'm so confused and my head is hurting and my heart is pounding and I need help help help to save myself from the man with my secret red cord around his waist for all to see.

Meg comes to my rescue again, my very own saviour in servant form. "Lady Shaw," she whispers urgently, "tell your daughter to approach that man there. She's showing all the signs of being bewitched by him. Her reaction to his touch will show if he's one of her tormentors."

My mind is hazy, but I understand Meg's words well enough and thank her silently for my deliverance. I don't need much urging from Mama to step up to John Lindsay of Barloch and grasp him by the hand. As soon as my skin touches his, I know what I must do. I understand well enough now my part in this play, and I act as though my immortal soul depends on my performance.

I drop to the floor, howling like the very winds of hell are whistling through me.

I'm so busy screaming and writhing on my back, I barely hear John's protests that he's done nothing to harm me. All I can see through my half-shut eyes is the red, red cord tied around his waist as Papa clamps his own hand around John's wrist and calls for the servants to fetch the Commissioners to come and question him.

Meg's not done protecting me yet – she flies at John Lindsay, accusing him of bewitching me and beating his chest with her fists, telling him to stop, stop stop. There's a tussle at the door to the library which Papa wins, locking John inside as much for his own safety as mine and telling Meg she's a faithful servant but she needs to attend to me now.

As she crouches down and cradles my head in her lap, I see her tucking the ends of the red cord into her apron and I know she's stolen my secret back and I'm safe safe safe in her gentle hands. My mind is shouting and the ravens are crying and there's nothing left in the world worth listening to except Meg's soft voice telling me to—

"Pull yourself together!"

Christian wrenched herself back into the present with an effort, ordering her wayward mind to do her bidding and stop wandering off. She took a deep breath and stepped into the pool of sunlight, letting the warm beams wash away the residue of unwanted memories. She was in control. She was mistress of her own destiny, and she had a job to do.

Feeling calmer, she reached out and turned the doorknob.

The library was cooler than the other rooms, with its row of high windows blocked by bleaching slates. Christian gripped the pieces of her stolen twist-mill in shaking hands, trying to draw strength from her visionary dream of twelve spindles of pure thread all being spun at once. She would revolutionise the industry here in Scotland. She would produce the strongest, whitest thread the world had ever seen. It was more than a dream. It was her destiny.

Revived by ambition, she strode with renewed purpose to the window, taking down her small test slate. The sunlight bleaching period for this batch of thread was over. It was time to assess the results. Half hopeful, half praying, Christian turned over the test slate.

The thread fixed there was no longer white. It was red, red, red and dripped with blood as though each strand was a pulsing vein ripped from the arm of a living victim.

Christian cried out in horror and dropped the slate. It crashed to the floor, shattering into pieces, the bloody thread oozing across the floorboards. She shut her eyes to escape the sight, but there was no escape from her own mind, the images whirling fast as a hurricane through her head.

The metal jaws bite and my blood runs red into the white bowl all stained with my guilt and sin and I'm begging for mercy and crying for help but all that comes out are the names of the people I'm afraid have guessed my secret.

Margaret Lang.

Katherine Campbell.

Agnes Naismith.

John and James Lindsay of Erskine.

John Lindsay of Barloch.

John Reid.

Maggie Fulton.

And others, and others and others, so many names that fly from my lips like ravens screeching from the rooftops and circling in the sky grown so dark and cloudy I can barely see. They're guilty. Not guilty. Guilty. Not guilty. Of what? I don't know anymore, I just want it all to be over.

Christian gasped, her nails digging into her palms so hard they pierced the skin. Running from the room without looking back at the fallen slate and the bloody thread, she sought sanctuary in the spinning room, where Bess and Janet's loosely spun strands of linen were waiting on spindles for her clever hand to turn into strong, fine thread. But when she opened the door, she found no peace or respite there. The wheels were turning all on their own, the treadles pumped up, down, up, down by some unseen force as the bloody red thread ran in rivers from the wheels and twisted round the spindles in sticky clumps of gore.

"Mistress Shaw?"

Slamming the door so no one else could see inside, Christian whirled round. Meg was standing at the top of the stairs, her eyes wide with concern.

"Is everything alright, Mistress Shaw? Can I get you anything?"

"I'm fine, thank you Meg." Christian said, forcing her voice to remain steady despite her hammering heart. "I'm a little tired from sitting up with my sister all night. Perhaps you could air my linen and freshen up the dress I was wearing when the minister called this morning?"

Meg didn't need to be told what Christian was really asking. The maid was carrying a basket of freshly laundered sheets that she'd carried to the river at sunrise and washed there before anyone could see. It was a tightly held secret known only to her family that Christian didn't bleed as other women did, and one that, if previously known, would have ended any hopes of her ever being married. Even the taint of the witch trials would have been nothing to the knowledge that she was barren. But Christian had such a perverse fear of anyone seeing this returning proof of her womanhood that Meg knew better than to let the other servants catch a glimpse of the stained linen.

"Of course, Mistress Shaw, I'll see to it at once."

Meg's the only one I can trust in this madhouse! Christian thought as she hurried down the stairs and out into the courtyard. *She's the only one here who can help me.*

But despite the faith she placed in her loyal friend and confidant, Christian couldn't tell her about the visions she was seeing. She couldn't bear the thought that her past might be repeating itself. Meg would see witchcraft at its root... *and then there'll be accusations, and confessions, and clergy and commissions, and before I know it I'll be standing on the Gallow Green again while the executioner pulls his rope tight and the fires are lit and—*

Pull yourself together! Christian shouted above the child's voice that was ringing through her head. *You can't give in to this silly weakness, you have work to do!*

She knew she shouldn't work on a Sunday, but her thread came before everything else. It was time to remove the new batch from their buttermilk barrels, and with the servants busy in the kitchen and bedrooms, preparing food for the guests who would arrive next day from Edinburgh, helping the doctor attend to Elizabeth, and comforting Jean and Lady Shaw, there were no free hands to help her with her own work.

I can do it myself, she thought resolutely. I *will drag this family back up to its rightful position, even if it costs me my last breath.*

Marching to the bleaching barn, she prised open the lid of the first barrel, determined to drain and wash the whole batch of thread and begin the sunlight bleaching process herself.

The buttermilk was not white as she hoped, nor curdled yellow as she feared. The barrel was filled to the brim with blood, the soaking thread swilling around the rancid mix like discarded sinews on the floor of a slaughterhouse.

Christian gasped in horror and turned her face to the wall.

I've had this vision before. It won't last. I just have to look away, and when I look back it will all be—

But it wasn't over, and it wasn't all right. When she looked again, the buttermilk was still a churning soup of carnage, the blood bubbling over the edges of the barrel to pool on the floor.

A strangled howl shook her to the core, and Christian put her hands to her ears, the crying of ravens on the rooftops rising to fever pitch. The air seemed to rush from her lungs, and she staggered to the door, panting for breath. Gazing up at the sky, she saw the black-winged birds circling in a huge dark cloud above the house, their beaks wide open as they screeched in warning.

Warning me of what?

The cloud parted, the midday sun dazzling her for a moment. When she opened her eyes again she could see the yellow rays flashing like fire on the windows, the ravens now a billow of smoke curling into the air.

Like fire..?

Christian blinked, and her blood ran cold. The light flickered and flashed in the windows, yellow, orange and red tongues licking their way up the wood and stonework. This was no product of an overwrought mind nor fantasy of an overtired body. She could smell the acrid tang of smoke and feel the heat of the blaze on her pale face.

This vision was real.

Bargarran House was burning.

Warp:

Thursday 10th June 1697

I don't want to be here be here be here...

But I have no choice. Papa says I must watch the witches burn so I'll know that justice has been done and they can't hurt me anymore. The men with metal jaws have stopped biting me and I'm much better, so now I wonder if it wasn't all just a bad dream and if the people I've condemned really deserve what's coming. But then I remember the red rags and the eyes that spied out my secrets, and I'll know I'll never be safe till the flames have eaten their fill and the witches' flesh is black as ravens' wings.

I want to stay at the back of the crowd, but Papa takes us right up to the front, pushing the labourers aside with his riding crop and saying 'excuse me' to the well-dressed ladies. The jailers are chaining the six prisoners to stakes just as we get to the front of the crowd. I accused so, so many when the metal jaws were biting my arm and spilling my blood and draining my reason into that white bowl of madness, but in the end it was just seven the Commission chose to kill.

John Reid's not here.

He hanged himself in his cell rather than face the crowd and the rope and the flames, and now he's dead and buried and his beautiful body's being eaten by worms and his lovely dark eyes are just holes where the maggots are nesting.

It's not my fault my fault my fault…

I grit my teeth and clutch Meg's arm and try not to look at the accusing eyes that are staring back at me as the witches are chained to the stakes. Katherine Campbell's screaming like the ravens on the rooftops and fighting the jailers so hard I'm sure her bones are snapping like dry tinder as they chain her up. John Lindsay of Barloch's already tied so tight he can't raise his hands to ears, so he's got his eyes screwed shut instead like that will somehow stop him from hearing his wife's terrible wailing from the watching crowd. Maggie Fulton's lost her mind with hunger and lack of sleep and she's prattling on and on about the fairy horses that are going to carry her off to elf land where she'll be queen of all the little magic people and live in luxury all her days. The Lindsay brothers are chained together, holding each other close like babes in arms and not grown men, and Margaret Lang's shaved head is bowed and she's praying, praying, praying.

Agnes Naismith's looking straight at me, her red-rimmed eyes seeing all my sins like I'm made of glass and she knows she knows she knows that my rags were red that day and what the red cord round my wrist in the sunrise was for even though I've just got a big black hole in my head where the memory of my deeds once was.

Katherine Campbell's screaming 'liar, liar, liar' at me until the executioner puts his rope around her neck and pulls like it's the red, red cord and she twitches and jerks till it's all, all over and she'll never curse me or whisper wicked words in my ears ever again. The black-hooded man passes down the line undoing the work the raven woman did in the dark long ago, but I don't watch as I can't take my eyes off the old woman who's drilling a fresh hole in my mind with her stare full of anger and sorrow and pity and hate.

I'm sorry I'm sorry I'm sorry...

But it's too late for that as the black-hooded man's putting his rope around Agnes Naismith's throat and she's shouting at me 'May you never know peace until the day you die'!' And then she's gasping and twitching and gurgling and dying and the only thing left moving is the monstrous raven that swoops down to land on her stake ready to peck at her eyes before the fires are lit and the tasty flesh is all blackened and burned.

I don't want to watch this watch this watch this...

But Papa's gripping my arm as the kindling and tar

is piled up around the stakes and the executioner lights the pyres. The fire spreads to my mind and fills it with smoke, and soon I don't know if the melting flesh that's making me retch is all in my mind or if my nightmare's real.

This can't be happening happening happening...

I know it can't as the raven hasn't moved, it's just sitting there at the top of the stake as the flames climb high into the sky. It's not screeching or flapping around in the fire, instead it's looking straight at me with eyes as black as coals and a smile on its beak as knowing and cunning as the one Katherine Campbell wore when she whispered her wicked words in the dark and sent my mind spinning down into hell.

Weft:

Sunday 10th June 1722

"Mary! Bess! Janet! Fire!" Christian cried as she raced back into the house, heedless now of the barrels of blood in the barn and the red rags she should take more care to keep secure. "Fetch the sand buckets – there's a fire in the library!"

The kitchen maid stared at her dumbly with her mouth open, but the two young spinners having their lunch at the kitchen table sprang into action. Running up the stairs, Janet went to warn the rest of the house, while Bess made straight for the library, grabbing the bucket of sand standing in the hallway for emergencies and calling for Mary to fetch water. Christian tried to keep up, but the bundle of rags stuffed in her undergarments chafed her legs, shifting out of place and threatening to leak her secret if she moved any faster.

"Bess, be careful! This whole side of the house is ablaze!" Christian called as the servant pulled the door open. A wave of heat hit Christian full in the face, sucking the air from her lungs and scorching her skin. The smell of burnt flesh was sickening, and for a moment she thought the young spinner had been consumed by the flames.

The fires are raging and the witches are burning but even though they're dead I can still hear them screaming in my head and cursing me every which way to hell, or maybe it's just the ravens as now there's more than one circling above me, there's a whole army of them sent from hell to—

"Widow Millar?"

Christian opened her stinging eyes to see Bess gazing into the library and then back at her, a puzzled look on her face.

"You said there was a fire..?"

Christian blinked. The library was as still and peaceful as a graveyard, the blocked windows throwing the room into shadow. There was no fire here, no flames ripping through the house and turning her family home to ashes.

"I thought…"

She took a hesitant step into the cool, silent room, searching the floor for the broken test slate and the bloody threads she'd dropped earlier. The brown oak of the worn boards was untarnished by the gory pool she'd seen spread across it a short time ago, no fragments of shattered slate to be seen. Glancing up, she stifled a gasp.

The test slate was back in place in the window, smooth and whole as if it had never been touched.

She'd imagined the whole thing.

No! That's not possible! I saw—

"Christian? Is everything alright?" Her mother's voice was thin and trembling, as though one more shock would break her in half. Christian gradually became aware of the press of bodies in the hall. The whole household looking in at her, their eyes wide with fear and wonder. "Janet says you saw a fire..?"

There were questions in everyone's eyes and on everyone's lips, questions that Christian couldn't answer. "I was mistaken," she said stiffly, trying to pull herself back together. "The sun must have dazzled me for a moment."

"That's not surprising, Mistress Shaw, given how hard you've been working since the accident and how little sleep you've had." Meg came to her rescue yet again, shooing the other servants back to their chores, and reassuring her mother and Jean that everything was alright.

"Would you like me to make you up a sleeping draught, Widow Millar?" the doctor asked, frowning at her in concern. He'd clearly been dozing in his chair by Elizabeth's bed, as his shirt was crumpled and he was struggling to stifle a yawn now that the panic was over. Christian couldn't blame him. She suddenly felt so tired it was an effort to stay upright.

"No, thank you, I'm quite alright," she lied, leaning back against the wall so the others wouldn't see her legs trembling.

"Well, if you're sure…"

The doctor went back to his patient, and her mother and Jean went back to their mourning, and finally Christian was left in peace with the one woman she trusted not to use her temporary weakness as a weapon against her.

"You should rest, Mistress Shaw," Meg urged. "You'll need your strength for what's coming."

"What's coming..? Oh, you mean Alexander Murray's odious sister and her family arriving tomorrow. Yes, that will be a trial. But never mind that, Meg, I need you to do something for me."

"Anything, Mistress Shaw."

Christian's head was spinning, and she struggled to get the words out. "Make sure there's not a single fire lit in this house tonight. I can't explain it, but there mustn't be flames – no flames… Do you hear me?"

"Yes, Mistress Shaw. But the supper tonight, surely..?"

"I said no flames! Not even a candle. Do you understand?" Christian could hear her voice flying out of control, the notes high-pitched and hysterical.

"I'll make sure of it, Mistress Shaw." Meg withdrew to issue orders to the other servants, leaving Christian to gather her scattered thoughts. Beyond the open doorway, the library was no longer silent and still, but filled with the memory of ravens, each echo louder than the one before. They were no longer crying, wailing or screeching. Now, they seemed to be laughing.

Clutching her crucifix so hard that it hurt her palms, Christian slammed the door shut and ran to her room, throwing herself down by the side of her bed to pray as if her very life depended on it.

Our Father, white shirts and linen…

No, that wasn't right. She shut her eyes tighter, trying again.

Hollow be thy name. The raven's come, thy will's undone, and there is no Heaven…

Christian felt a cold hand of fear shiver down her spine as she searched for the words that had once been so familiar, and found only a tangle of barbed phrases in their place.

Give us this day our rags so red…

No!

Give us this day our pure white thread…

With a cry of despair, Christian leapt to her feet and snatched up the bible that lay on her bedside table. Tying her green plaid around her waist, she marched out, reading aloud as she paced through the hallways and corridors, searching for the faith that had abandoned her just as she needed it the most.

The clergy are all gathered round my bed firing questions at me, and I'm scared if I miss even one then my story of the witches will be blown to bits and I'll be condemned as a liar. They make me recite my Catechism and repeat the Psalms and tell the parables all in order and I know they're testing me to see if the devil's got in and I have to be strangled and burned along with the people I've named to the Commission. I've been a good, good girl and learned my lessons well at church and give them every answer they need to hear to save my soul and all the while I'm praying so hard it hurts, it hurts, it hurts…

"Mistress Shaw, please will you take some supper?" Meg's calming voice broke into her fevered thoughts at last. "Everyone's afeared for your health but no one's dared disturb you until now. The family's all abed and the servants have turned in, so it's only you and me still up so late."

"Late? But it was only midday a moment ago…" Christian gazed down the darkened hall, puzzled to find it lit by moonlight instead of the rays of the sun.

"You've been wandering around for hours and hours, Mistress Shaw, and babbling such nonsense words we were half afraid the horse had maybe struck at your head too without us knowing."

"Nonsense words? No, I was reading from my bible."

"That's not what we heard, mistress."

Clutching her crucifix so hard that it hurt her palms, Christian slammed the door shut and ran to her room, throwing herself down by the side of her bed to pray as if her very life depended on it.

Christian's blood ran cold, and she peered at the words she's been reading. They ran together like rivers of red blood on a white page, and she dropped the book in disgust.

"Let's get you to bed, Mistress Shaw, you've overtired yourself of late."

"Yes, I think I need to… Meg? What's that light? I thought I told you there were to be no candles and no fires lit?"

Before the maid could answer, Christian rushed down the hall. There was a sliver of light coming from under Elizabeth's door, and the tell-tale smell of a fire burning in the grate sent Christian's mind into spirals of panic.

The fires are burning, burning, burning and they're red as my shame and turning the witches' flesh black as my sins and there's nowhere to hide from the eyes of the raven that's circling, circling, circling the killing grounds where the crowds are baying for blood…

"Jean! What are you doing?"

Throwing open the door, Christian was horrified to see her youngest sister leaning over the fire in the grate, heaping more logs onto the blaze. Elizabeth was moaning in bed, her maid clutching her hand and trying to coax her back to sleep. The doctor was clearly sleeping in the guest room down the hall, as his chair by the bed was empty and Jean had taken over his watch for the night.

"The ravens!" Jean cried, her eyes wide with panic. "They've got the devil in them, Christian! They're trying to come down the chimney!"

"What?" Christian rushed to the window and threw open the curtains. Outside on the windowsill, an army of birds stared back at her. As their eyes met, the ravens opened their beaks, sending up a terrible wail that howled round the house like the winds of winter. Christian tugged the curtains shut again to block out the horrible sight, but she couldn't escape the awful sound as she rushed to the fire to help pile on more fuel. She could hear a desperate fluttering and scraping from the top of the chimney, as though there was something up there trying to escape the heat of the flames.

May you never know peace until the day you die!

Agnes Naismith's curse was coming true, the punishment for her sins carried on the wings of the ravens who'd watched Christian her whole life and found her wanting.

"Meg, rouse the others! Tell them to light every fire in the house!" Christian yelled.

"But, Mistress Shaw, you said—"

"Just do it! And don't forget the kitchen and the spinning room."

Meg didn't argue, and Christian could hear her footsteps pattering down the hall above the wild cries of the ravens.

"Keep piling on logs, and when you're done here, go and help Meg and the others light the rest of the fires."

"Christian, where are you going?" Jean cried as her sister ran for the door.

"I need to light the fire in the back sitting room, the others won't think of that."

"But Alexander's in there! You have to keep that room cool!"

Christian ran on without a backward glance. She knew as she raced down the stairs that her unchanged rags were soaked through and staining her dress, but she didn't care anymore. Her shame was nothing to the fear of the birds that had haunted her every waking moment for twenty-five years.

Stumbling through the back corridor in the dark, she prayed the birds hadn't yet found this particular chimney as her hand grasped the doorknob and the door swung open. The curtains were not closed out of respect the way they had been before. Now they were gaping open, the full moon gleaming on the white shirt of the corpse laid out on the table.

The body the body the body is strangely soft under my

fingers as I run the washcloth over the smooth skin at the waist and let them explore the coarse hair that curls up from–

Christian's hands were shaking so hard she could barely strike the firesteel with the flint. Sparks flared once, twice, three times, but the small pile of kindling in the grate stubbornly refused to light. She could hear the scuffling and scraping sounds above her grow louder as though an army of winged creatures was trying to force themselves down the chimney all at once.

The kindling finally sparked and flared, and Christian doused the logs with the bottle of whisky she snatched from the side table before throwing them on the weak fire. At once the flames shot up, the logs blazing with sudden heat. An angry shrieking echoed from the flue, and Christian scrambled back as something came tumbling down in a hail of soot and ash. A huge black shape burst from the flames, its wings ablaze as it screeched round the room. At first Christian thought it was searching for an escape route, but then it found what it seeking, and it settled on Alexander Murray's corpse, its fiery wings singing the waxen figure's white shirt.

For moment, the corpse seemed to shimmer, and then it went up in flames, shocking Christian with the intensity of the heat and light the sudden burst produced. The smell of charred flesh made her retch, dragging buried memories up from the deep holes in her mind.

The witches' flesh is burning, burning, burning and I'm being sick on my shoes because the smell makes me think of the whole roast ox our cook prepared in the kitchen last week to celebrate me being well again and it makes my mouth water when I remember the sweet taste of the tender meat. I don't want to think of feasting while I watch the people I've condemned consumed by flames, as it just confirms that I'm wicked, wicked, wicked and will one day burn in hell myself for all I've done.

Christian fell to her knees, weak with horror as the corpse on the table shivered and shook, blood oozing from its empty eye sockets to drip, drip, drip onto the floor like sizzling gobs of juice from the kitchen spit. As she watched the terrible scene, her own eyes wide with fright, the crucifix around Christian's neck suddenly flared white hot, scorching her skin and biting deep into her neck where the heavy chain hung. Before she could stop herself, she'd yanked it off, throwing the glowing metal into the fire.

At once the blazing light died, plunging the room into such sudden darkness that Christian was afraid she'd gone blind. Then the roiling clouds parted, the full moon shining down to illuminate the ghostly scene. The snuffed fire was smoking in the grate, but the scrambling sounds in the chimney had gone, no new invaders forcing their way down into the room. Turning back to the table, Christian saw the corpse laid out as fresh and spotless as it had been when she first entered. There was no scorched linen, no burned flesh.

There was only a great black raven sitting on the dead man's chest, watching Christian with glistening eyes. Cocking its head to one side, it opened its beak wide, the strange infant's wail that filled the room a question this time, instead of an accusation.

Christian's shaking limbs were stilled, her pounding heart slowing until it seemed like her blood had turned to pure ice, numbing her to the inevitable surrender. She'd prayed and bargained and begged for twenty-five years, but it was no use. There was no escaping her past. She would have to face the truth now, or accept madness and delusion as her fate.

"I'm ready," she whispered, her voice a low croak that answered the raven's high-pitched cry. She opened the sitting room door, watching with unblinking eyes as the raven unfurled its great wings and flew off down the hallway. Christian followed, each footstep a dull thump of resignation as she crossed to the kitchen door.

A few minutes later, Meg came downstairs to check on her mistress, her calls echoing through the empty corridors. Seeing the back door ajar, she stepped into the courtyard just in time to see Christian mounting the family's fastest horse and riding off across the moonlit fields, her hair streaming behind her as she followed the flight of a great black bird in the sky high above.

Warp:

Thursday 10th June 1697

The fires have died but the smell still lingers over the Gallow Green. I thought I'd be taken home as soon as the burnings were done, but Papa's made us wait all day till the bitter end when the witches' remains will be buried and the horseshoe over the burial mound fixed in place. The smoke's been blown away by the breeze, but there's a black cloud circling above the execution ground that makes me shiver every time I turn my head to look back, and there's a wailing, wailing, wailing on the wind that stirs restless memories of red cords and dead babes strangled in the night.

Our horse and cart stops behind the wagon that's carrying the witches' remains, and Papa makes me stand up so I can see over the heads of the people who've gathered to watch the charred corpses being imprisoned in the ground. I grip Meg's hand for comfort as the grave diggers toss the bodies into the deep pit on top of the mouldering corpse of John Reid that's been lying at the bottom for weeks now. There's no pure white winding sheets and no minister praying over the remains. There's just the jeers of the crowd who spit and throw rotten food to send the condemned witches on their way down, down, down to the everlasting fires of hell.

"Courage, Mistress Shaw, it will all be over soon," Meg tells me, and I want to believe her but my mind's starting to unravel and my vision's going dark, and I don't know if it's hunger or if night's drawing in now the sky's so full of restless clouds. The crowd is cheering, and I look back out over Maxwellton Cross where the grave diggers have finished their work and are fixing a horseshoe over the burial mound to ward the spot where the witches are resting. Papa says the iron will keep the witches from rising, but after everything that's happened with the doctors and their metals jaws and bowls of bloody madness, and the Commission with their questions and their witch prickers prodding, prodding, prodding, I don't know if I can trust a single thing he says ever again.

I know he's guessed that I'm losing my faith, but he thinks that it's my faith in God that's wavering, as he bends down and draws a heavy crucifix from his pocket. "This belonged to my mother, and her mother before her," he tells me as he hangs it round my neck. "I wanted to give it to you before now, but I had to make sure every trace of the witches' influence over you was gone, else it would harm rather than help you."

I want to feel happy and reassured as he gets down from the cart to go and talk to the clergy who've gathered to watch the burial, but all I feel is a sick dread in the pit of my stomach and a nagging feeling of guilt that the heavy metal cross somehow makes worse. But Jesus had his cross to bear and now I have mine, so I swallow the bile and pray for deliverance and smile at the people throwing me suspicious looks as they head back home.

Papa comes back with the clergy and they tell me we all need to go to the burial mound to say a prayer of thanks to God for delivering us from the witches, but my knees shake so hard at the thought that Papa has to lift me down from the cart and half carry me over to the unholy site. The adults all bow their heads and close their eyes while the oldest minister drones on and on and on in endless prayer, but my eyes are wide, wide open, watching the black stain that's rolling across the sky.

It's not smoke, and it's not a real cloud either. It's a flock of ravens, the kind of big gathering that Meg calls an unkindness or a treachery when they're wheeling high above Bargarran House on winter's day. It's a summer night now, but the wind seems to blow just as cold as they come circling, circling, circling over the clergy's bowed heads. One peels off from the rest of the group and comes to land on the burial mound, and somehow I know, I know, I know as it stares right through me that this is the one that sat on Agnes Naismith's stake as she cursed me and robbed me of any chance of future peace.

Pilate washed his hands of his wickedness, but when I look down at my own they're black with soot and red where I've clutched my crucifix so hard it's bitten into my skin. I know I'm never going to be pure and spotless ever again even if my linen stays white and I never wrap the red, red cord around my wrist ever again.

The clergy are chanting and the ravens are crying, but the only sound in the whole world that I can hear is the soft whispered words of comfort Meg pours in my ear as she holds me tight and tells me that it's all, all right and nothing's going to hurt me ever again. Meg says she'll be there to protect me from the wickedness of the world and help me prosper as I grow, and she holds my soot-stained hand in hers as the night draws in and the black, black raven watches us from the burial mound with it all-seeing eyes.

Twisted Threads:

Sunday 10th June 1722 - Midnight

The horse is winded and panting by the time we reach Maxwellton Cross and my red, red rags are streaming down my thighs as I climb from the saddle, but I don't care as I just want all of this to be over, over, over.

The raven's sitting on the burial mound, and the horseshoe holding down the spirit of the witches has been pulled up and tossed aside. I know if I also want to be released from the curse I've been under for all these years I'll have to let it unlock my deepest memories and remember the reasons I hid them away in the first place. The streets are deserted at this late hour and there's no one to see me but this bird I'm sure is the very same one that sat on Agnes Naismith's stake and watched as the witches burned so long ago.

I haven't come here of my own free will, I've been summoned to answer for sins I've chosen to forget, and as I kneel on the scrubby grass and meet the raven's gaze, I can feel the floodgates of my mind opening. I plunge deep under water and watch an image form on the surface as the froth of my mind clears.

I'm eleven years old, but somehow I'm not a child, as I'm seeing through the eyes of the adults I'd go on to accuse. Margaret Lang's just an ordinary midwife, her red rag tied to the bed as a silly superstition she was taught by the women who came before her. She only wants to help, but there's a girl watching from the doorway where she shouldn't be, a girl who sees all and understand nothing, a girl who goes running off into the night to cry in her room about rags and bundles until Katherine Campbell comes to console her. The Highland woman's hard as nails but soft in the centre, and she tells the girl truths that are meant to bring comfort and calm her fright, but all they do is stoke the fires of confusion till the girl's mind is running wild with fantasies and unfounded fears.

My lungs are burning as though I'm underwater, and I surface for a moment to draw in a long, shaky breath before the raven plunges me into the roiling cauldron of memories once more.

I'm eleven again, and not a child for sure, as there's blood on my rags and a fear of discovery that runs so deep to my roots it fragments my mind and drives me to madness. For a moment I glimpse a girl wearing a white nightdress stained with blood as she stands over first one crib, then another and another, and unwraps a red cord that's around her wrist and undoes wicked deeds done in the dark and the raven woman's work by candlelight.

In that terrible moment I know what I've done, and I scream out loud with the horror of it. But there's more, there's more, and before I can catch my breath, the raven's sent me diving back down to the bottom of that murky pool of memories.

I see the people I've condemned one by one through the eyes of the child-woman, each heedless of my sins and my shame as they go about their own business, their only crime being unfortunate enough to cross paths with me when the fear was upon me and the madness was at its peak. The images tumble over each other, faster and faster as I see the doctors who tried to help and unwittingly sent me spiralling further into delusion, the clergy with their superstitions and need for importance goading me to name more and more people to fuel the fire of their investigation that ends in real flames for seven of the condemned and in death for all.

"I'm sorry!" I gasp, "I'm sorry I'm sorry I'm sorry." I hold out my hands to ask for forgiveness, but they're stained red with blood and they drip onto the burial mound where the ashes of the falsely accused lie, and the crimson patch on my dress is blooming in the dark in accusation. The raven hasn't finished with me yet, and sends me kicking and screaming back down to the depths where I see what I've done to my own sister and the other's suitor in a moment of madness to escape discovery. A horse rears up; one body falls and another is broken, lives are ruined but secrets preserved. And all the while, Jean is sobbing, sobbing, sobbing through the corridors of my mind that are echoing with all the suffering I've caused my family.

As I surface again it all becomes clear, and I see now I was never cursed – the curse was me and myself and my madness-tinged mind. I crawl forward on buckling knees, my blood-stained hands clasped in pleading now. "How do I atone?" I sob, my will broken and my body all atremble. "How do I fix all the misery and hurt and gain peace?"

Make it stop make it stop make it stop, my mind is wailing. I'll do anything anything anything.

It's this silent plea that the raven responds to. Its all-seeing eyes glitter and it plucks a feather from its wing, placing it in my outstretched hand. I see black on red on white, and there's a blinding flash in my mind as though moonlight on snowfall and sunlight on water have all merged into the images that ripple before my eyes.

The world is made of pure white linen, an abundant flowering of ladies' caps, baby bonnets and christening robes spread out as far as the eye can see. The wind catches at the petals, sending wedding gowns, night shirts and handkerchiefs billowing out to the four corners of the Earth, their beautiful threads so white white white it makes my heart bleed with longing to watch as they flutter away. At the centre of it all is me and my industry-defining machine, my wondrous twelve spindled hand-cranked twist mill that sets a production standard others can only dream of attaining.

"How?" I cry, my voice trembling with hope and desire. "How do I get my thread so white? How do I achieve such a spotless state?"

The answer to both questions is the same. The raven raises its beak, waiting.

I know who and what this bird is, and why it's been circling me all these years. I dared not admit it to myself until now, but the curtain has been lifted on my mind and the show of illusion is over. It's either my eternal soul or my earthly mind – damnation or madness – and I sealed my fate as a not-quite-child with the red, red cord and the words of accusation that brought the fires of hell raging from the deep to burn the bodies of the innocent.

I'm damned already, I have nothing more to lose. "You'll give me peace and prosperity, if I pledge my allegiance, and give you my soul, such as it is?" I ask, my voice trembling with fear and hope.

Another image flashes through my mind in response, a whirling of strong white thread, finer and purer than any the world has ever seen, embroidered in heartbreakingly beautiful decorations on snowy lawn and cambric.

"And my family?" I ask, one last question to settle before the point of no return. "Will they prosper?"

I see Mama walking through Paisley with her head held high, everyone smiling and nodding to her in deference. Jean's the belle of the ball in her dazzling white dress, and Elizabeth's by my side in the spinning room, the dull glaze of imbecility in her eyes belied by the speed her hands work now that her wicked tongue's been silenced by the horse's lunging hooves.

I've seen enough. I know the future I have to choose.

"Then I accept," I say, a sigh of relief and resignation that shivers on the wind before being carried off into the night. I hold out my hand again, and the raven brings its beak down sharply on my palm, drawing blood for real. As the red, red, drops drip onto the burial mound, I can feel the flow between my thighs dry up, the stain on my dress disappearing, leaving me pure and spotless, but not innocent – no, not that. I have eaten from the fruit of the tree of knowledge, and as I gaze at the black feather mixed with red blood on my white palm, I finally have the piece of the bleaching puzzle I've been missing.

All this time I've been washing my thread with white soap, trying to cleanse my sins with something pure. I was wrong. It's black soap I should have been using all along, as nothing perfect can ever be produced without the harsh taint of sacrifice. I kiss the feather with grateful lips and feel the weight of my sins lifting. I've been absolved, at least for now, and for the whole course of my life I'll never be troubled by blood, or guilt or visions again. What comes after that, I cannot say, but for now, the temporary reprieve is enough.

"Mistress Shaw? It's time to go home. We have work to do."

I look up in surprise. Meg is standing over me, offering me her hand, but how she got here I don't know, as there's no other horse in the street but the one I rode. I turn to the burial mound, but the raven is gone, and the horseshoe is back in place, undisturbed. The story of the witches will remain the one that I told twenty-five years before, and nothing will ever again disturb the resting ground where the innocent condemned are entombed.

I take Meg's outstretched hand and we mount my horse, and in that moment it all becomes clear. I finally understand the real history that will never be spoken aloud, but will be spun into the future of the thread industry I'll build here in Paisley, a legacy to outlast all others.

Meg smiles at me, and there's a red smear of blood around her lips that drips onto her dress as black as night. Her fingers are feathers and her arms are wings that encircle me, holding me tight, binding me to her, and now I know who the real raven woman is as we ride together past the spot on the Gallow Green where the witch fires consumed seven sacrificial souls in a bonfire of innocence. I'm under Meg's protection, under her spell, and as long as I do her bidding I'll never have to be afraid of anything again. My sins have bought the Devil's secret, and one day soon, I'll have the purest white thread the world has ever seen.

Afterword

Although the events portrayed in *Red Runs the Witch's Thread* are fictional, the story is based on the real-life witch trials which took take in Paisley in 1697, when eleven-year-old Christian Shaw accused thirty-five local people of bewitching her, seven of whom were strangled and burned at the stake in June 1697. This proved to be the last mass burning of witches in Europe, and Christian Shaw did indeed go on to become a successful businesswoman, establishing the Bargarran Thread Company which became a prosperous business by the end of the 1720s. When she was buried in Greyfriars Kirkyard in Edinburgh in 1737, the story of the Bargarran witches died with her, but her legacy lived on for over two centuries in the form of the thriving Paisley thread industry to which her early innovations had contributed so much.

Today, the movement demanding a formal pardon for those accused and convicted of the crime of witchcraft is growing in Scotland. In 2022, Scotland's First Minister issued an apology to people accused during the time of the Witchcraft Act which was in force in Scotland between 1563 and 1736. As of April 2023 when *Red Runs the Witch's Thread* was first published, the campaign for a legal pardon and a national monument for the estimated 3837 people who were accused of witchcraft – many of whom were executed – is ongoing.

About the author

Victoria Williamson is an award-winning author who grew up in Scotland surrounded by hills, books, and an historical farm estate which inspired many of her early adventure stories and spooky tales. After studying Physics at the University of Glasgow, she set out on her own real life adventures, which included teaching maths and science in Cameroon, training teachers in Malawi, teaching English in China, and working with children with additional support needs in the UK.

Victoria has a deep interest in local history and archaeology, and regularly takes part in digs with Archaeology Scotland. Her previous historical children's novels, *Hag Storm* and *The Whistlers in the Dark*, have explored the life of Robert Burns in eighteenth century Scotland as well as Roman Scotland at the Antonine Wall in 158 AD. Her adult novellas, *The Haunting Scent of Poppies*, and *Red Runs the Witch's Thread* combine her love of history with her fascination with supernatural tales, and are perfect for reading by the fire on cold, dark days.

strangelymagical.com

@strangelymagic

Printed in Great Britain
by Amazon

38371970R00101